When the door opened and he stood there, tall, chocolate and fine, she was at a loss for words. Who was this tanned Adonis with the brown eyes?

"Yes?" he asked, his voice melodic and his smile hypnotizing.

"U-um, I'm your neighbor," Mimi stammered. "I didn't know someone had moved in and I was…Well, I was being nosy."

He smiled again as he gave her a cool once-over. Mimi wished that she had already dressed in her party clothes instead of the Atlanta basketball tank top and the pair of formfitting black leggings she still wore. "If you're the welcoming committee, where are the cupcakes and muffins?" he quipped.

"I said I was nosy, not a cook. Besides, you don't look as if you let carbs touch your lips," she said, then zeroed in on his flat midsection, which she imagined held a set of washboard abs.

"Wouldn't say that. I know how to work them off," he replied.

"I bet you do," she muttered.

"I'm sorry?"

"Mimi Collins. I'm Mimi Collins, and you are?"

"Brent Daniels," he said, then extended his hand. Mimi took his hand and sizzling jolts of electric lust flowed through her body.

Dear Reader,

They say opposites attract, and in the case of Mimi and Brent, there is no truer statement. Mimi Collins is the kind of woman who speaks first and deals with consequences later. That's easy to do when you're a blogger looking for hits on your website.

As far as Brent Daniels is concerned, he needs a carefully crafted image to get out of his father's shadow. So when these two collide, one has to wonder, how will their different ideas on life and love lead them to that magical moment?

It was such an adventure to write about oil and water actually mixing and working. I hope you enjoy the journey of Mimi and Brent as they steam things up between the pages.

Cheris

Feel
the
Heat

CHERIS HODGES

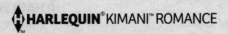
HARLEQUIN® KIMANI™ ROMANCE

Recycling programs
for this product may
not exist in your area.

ISBN-13: 978-0-373-86488-1

Feel the Heat

Printed in U.S.A.

Cheris Hodges was bit by the writing bug early. The 1999 graduate of Johnson C. Smith University is a freelance journalist and always looks for love stories in the most unusual places. She lives in Charlotte, North Carolina, where she is trying and failing to develop a green thumb.

Books by Cheris Hodges

Harlequin Kimani Romance

Blissful Summer with Lisa Marie Perry
Feel the Heat

Chapter 1

Mimi Collins pressed the post button on her blog and all she heard was her best friend, Michael Jane, affectionately known as MJ, screaming.

"You have officially lost your mind," she said. "This is worse than my mother misspelling Michelle and naming me Michael! You do realize that Fast Love is going to come after you when they read this."

Mimi shrugged as she read over her post about the horrific dating event she'd attended the week before. Fast Love billed itself as the last site singles ever needed to log on to in order to find love.

What a bunch of bull. The Fast Love Mix and Mingle, which was held at SkyLounge in Atlanta, turned out to be casting call for "let's have a one-night stand." The first two men who'd approached her held conversations with her breasts; the third man just came out and asked her when she planned to get naked for him, then he'd flashed her a wad of cash. She'd been offended and confused, so Mimi approached some of the other women who'd been invited to the event. Their stories had mirrored hers.

When Mimi had headed to the bar, she'd noticed a man sitting alone nursing a whiskey sour.

"Did you find what you were looking for?" she'd asked as she waved for the bartender.

He rolled his eyes at her and grumbled no. "This isn't what I expected from the email Fast Love sent," he'd replied, then took a long sip of his drink.

"What was in your email?"

"Hot girls looking for action."

"Seriously?"

Nodding, he'd opened the mail app on his smartphone and showed her the Fast Love email. Mimi's mouth dropped at the image of half-naked women underneath the headline: Hot Girls Willing to Do Whatever... Fast Love Dating Event.

"What in the..." Mimi waved for the bartender, again. She needed a drink. She asked the man to forward her the email.

"What's in it for me?" he'd asked as he wiggled his eyebrows.

Narrowing her eyes at him, Mimi asked him if his wife knew where he was, then nodded toward his left hand and the telltale tan line on his ring finger.

"Whatever," he said, then agreed to forward her the email. After downing her single-malt scotch, Mimi headed over to a group of women who looked as if they were about to leave. After introducing herself as a relationship blogger, she asked them if they would share their thoughts about the event and why they'd signed up for Fast Love.

Two of the three women agreed to talk, and her story was born.

"Mariah Danielle Collins!" MJ said, breaking into her thoughts. "Are you listening to me?"

"Nope," Mimi replied. "And the post is already getting hits." She turned her computer screen toward MJ. "Look! Five thousand hits in ten minutes. This is going to be epic. Let's go celebrate."

MJ shook her head. "As a brand manager, I know that Fast Love isn't going to take this sitting down. And you have to think about your own brand! Hello, you are a *New York Times* bestselling author and we're in the middle of contract negotiations. You can't have this kind of publicity. This is going to be so ugly. *So* ugly."

"Nothing I said was a lie. They should've done a better job marketing this event. It was like a one-sided meat market. I'm doing the world a favor by exposing this nonsense. Too many people exploit single women to make money, and Fast Love is just another one of those companies. Like that obnoxious radio host who has been married four times but is supposed to be a relationship expert."

MJ cleared her throat. "And some people have labeled you the same, and I don't see you saying that you aren't an expert."

Mimi threw up her hands. "I'm a lifestyle blogger and author."

"And when that cable news network asked you to speak about dating in the digital age, I didn't hear you tell Bianca Norman that you weren't an expert."

"Listen," Mimi said, "that was the producer's job to get her straight. And I'm not an expert."

"Tell me something I don't know," MJ quipped.

Mimi glanced at her computer and saw that her post had reached ten thousand views. "Guess who's about to go viral! Come on, let's go."

The two friends headed for the Buckhead Saloon, one of Mimi's favorite bars. She could always depend on the bartenders to hip her to the latest drinks and celebrity gossip in the city. She even had her own drink there, the aptly named Mimi Collins—a fruity version of a Tom Collins. Mimi's book, *Dating in Atlanta: The Mis-Adventures of Mimi Collins*, had given the place a huge buzz because many of the dates she'd written about had started there. And when one of the reality stars from the city had talked about Mimi's book and the bar in a popular magazine, the place became a bona fide hot spot. The owners knew they had Mimi to thank for that. This afternoon, though, MJ and Mimi were going to celebrate with some hot wings.

"Mimi," MJ said as they walked into the bar. "What if Fast Love doesn't take to kindly to your viral post? You have a lot going on right now. You have the movie and second book deal in the works, and this could derail all of that."

"You worry too much." She waved to her favorite bartender as she and MJ took their seats at the end of the bar.

"Mimi, girl," Lydia said as she poured two drinks. "You're blowing up today! I was going to sign up for Fast Love, but after reading your blog I'm glad I didn't. I can meet creeps right here for free."

Mimi turned to MJ. "I did a public service. Now,

what was that you were saying about Fast Love coming after me?"

Before MJ could answer, Mimi's cell phone rang. "Oh my goodness, it's World Wide News," Mimi said, then answered her phone.

Sweat poured from Brent Daniels's face as he and Jamal Carver, his best friend, lifted the sofa from the back of the moving truck. "Tell me again why you didn't hire movers?" Jamal asked as they maneuvered the sofa up the stairs of the condo complex.

"Because the movers were booked up today and I need my furniture," Brent grunted.

"So damned impatient! If I didn't like this sofa, I'd drop it on your feet."

"We're strong enough to do this. Besides, you could use the exercise."

"You know I can drop it and go home."

"All right, all right. Dinner's on me."

"That's a given." The men climbed the three stories and made it to Brent's front door.

"Why did you decide to move anyway?" Jamal asked.

"Tired of yard work," Brent joked. "Besides, I moved out to the burbs because I thought I'd be starting a family."

Jamal dropped his head. "I tried to warn you. Denisha Tate wasn't worth your lifestyle change."

Brent sucked his teeth. "Are you ever going to let that go?"

"Nope. Because you keep dating these paper broads."

"Here we go," Brent said as he unlocked the door.

"You want these women who have all of the right

papers. The Spelman graduates, the PhDs from Yale, the Links sisters…"

"Stop it."

"You need to stop it. You're so busy trying to craft a perfect life that you're not living. You're a litigating machine, but when you crawl out of your work hole, you're boring."

Brent shook his head. "I'm far from boring. I just choose not to run the streets like a college student looking to score."

"Hey, I resemble that remark. Dude, we're living in the land of plenty. Plenty of booty, plenty of breasts and plenty of women who are down for whatever. You'd know that if got out of your law office every now and then. As a matter of fact, we're going out tonight."

"I've got briefs to prepare."

"After all of the work I've just put in moving your bed and desk, we're going out tonight to have a good time."

Brent relented because he couldn't deny how much help Jamal had been in moving his stuff. There was a part of him that knew there was a lot of truth in what Jamal said. But he had to craft his life this way; being the son of one Georgia's most notorious lawyers who fell from grace made everything he did subject to scrutiny.

Did he push himself too hard? Maybe. But he never wanted anyone to ever mistake him for his womanizing father. So, he had a type, and if she stepped out of line, his next step was out the door. Brent couldn't help it that he needed someone who kept her business private to go along with the image he'd created for himself.

But lately, the women he'd met wanted nothing more than to be the next housewife of some reality show.

And his ex-girlfriend Denisha Tate had almost sucked him into her plan. Who knew the contract attorney wanted their relationship to play out on TV?

"Yo," Jamal said, snapping his fingers in Brent's face, "we're done, right?"

"Yeah. I'll unpack this later."

"All right then, we'll meet back here in an hour and I will show you the beauty of Buckhead nightlife." Jamal headed for the door, then turned around and gave his friend a stony look. "Now don't let me come back in here and find you're buried in a law book or a brief. Give it a break for a few days."

Brent chuckled. "Okay. I'll try. I will give you tonight because you had a brother's back with this move. No work."

Jamal nodded and headed out the door. Once he was alone, Brent walked over to the bay window looking over the city. Maybe this was the change that he needed.

Chapter 2

Mimi had a good day and she was looking forward to a quiet night. MJ had finally stopped harassing her about the viral blog post. The World Wide News interview had been a success and video snippets were being shared on Twitter and Facebook. And her blog was blowing up even more. MJ had gotten Mimi booked on the local TV station for the five-thirty newscast.

Now that work was over, Mimi was ready to let her curly hair down and relax. And by relax, she meant getting wrapped up in a good book.

"MJ," Mimi called from the terrace of her condo. "I really don't want to go to some loud nightclub this evening."

MJ walked onto the terrace holding two glasses of sweet tea. "Good, because we're going to the Jazz Spot. My client has turned that place into a hot spot in the city."

"Oh, that's what we're calling *him* now? 'My client'?" Mimi laughed and MJ narrowed her eyes at her.

"I can't with you. Nic and I have a professional relationship that works. Don't be a hater."

Mimi rolled her eyes and turned toward the picturesque view of downtown Atlanta. MJ stood beside her friend and handed her a glass of tea. Mimi took a sip of the tea and sighed.

"What's that all about?" MJ asked as she followed Mimi's glance.

Shrugging, she set her glass on the railing. "I guess I'm just a little tired."

MJ shook her head. "Bull. You're plotting something in that pretty little head of yours. I know you, Mimi."

"I'm bored."

MJ furrowed her brows. "Really?"

She nodded as she took a long sip of tea. "How long have we been in Atlanta?" Mimi asked. "Since undergrad, and we've been out of school for…"

"I clearly know how old we are. But you have a great base here."

Mimi folded her arms across her chest. "I want to experience something new. I want to travel and write about new things. I know it's popular, but this dating stuff is getting really old. What's the point? My blog is about adventure, but I'm in a rut. I don't want to write a follow-up to my book. What am I supposed to say? Dating in Atlanta still sucks rotten eggs?"

MJ shrugged and downed her tea. "I love Atlanta. Driving down 285 is an adventure for me. Where do you want to go?"

Mimi's eyes sparkled. "Dallas, New Orleans, New

York, Mexico. I just want to take a map, throw darts at it and go."

"And you don't think we're at the age where it's time to settle down?"

"Maybe you are—I mean, you have this client you want to nurture and stroke."

"Shut up! Anyway, I'm going to change my clothes and I'll be back in about an hour. Then we can talk rationally about why you shouldn't leave Atlanta."

Simply because she didn't want to start an argument, Mimi nodded and agreed that she'd consider it. But there was seriously nothing that could change her mind. She needed something new in her life and she was going to reach out and grab it.

Brent had already broken his promise to Jamal this weekend. After their early morning workout and plan to explore the new neighborhood, Brent returned home and started working. He'd spent the majority of the morning on the phone with his paralegal. Then half of the afternoon was dedicated to having her go through motions that he'd drafted two weeks ago. Brent liked to be ready for the unexpected in civil cases. And even though this one seemed to be open and shut, he wanted to make sure he had all the i's dotted and the t's crossed.

When his doorbell had chimed and he was dressed only in his basketball shorts and a white tank top, he was sure he was going to hear an earful from his buddy. "Give me a second," he said as he padded over to the door. Without looking through the peephole, he opened the door.

Mimi was just being nosy. She'd heard noise in what she thought was still an empty unit in the building. But when the door opened and he stood there, tall, chocolate and fine, she was at a loss for words. Who was this tanned Adonis with slate gray eyes?

"Yes?" he asked, his voice deep like a quiet storm DJ and his smile hypnotizing.

"Umm, I'm your neighbor," Mimi stammered. "I didn't know someone had moved in and I was… Well, I was being nosy."

He smiled again as he gave her a cool once-over. Mimi wished that she had already dressed in her party clothes instead of an Atlanta Hawks tank top and a pair of form-fitting black leggings. "If you're the welcoming committee, where are the cupcakes and muffins?" he quipped.

"I said I was nosy, not a cook. Besides, you don't look as if you let carbs touch your lips," she said, then zeroed in on a flat midsection that she imagined held a set of washboard abs.

"Wouldn't say that. I know how to work them off," he replied.

"I bet you do," she muttered.

"I'm sorry?"

"Mimi Collins. I'm Mimi Collins, and you are…?"

"Brent Daniels," he said, then extended his hand. Mimi shook it and sizzling jolts of electric lust flowed through her body. Tilting her head to the side, she focused on his face.

"Where do I know you from?" she asked. "You look very familiar."

He shrugged. "I'm an attorney."

It was as if a light bulb went off in her head. An attorney? He was the *attorney*! Brent Daniels was the man you called when you needed a one-lawyer dream team. And this was her neighbor?

"So, you're that Brent Daniels! Wow. Welcome to the neighborhood."

"I like the way you say my name," he said with another megawatt smile. Mimi inhaled sharply, her nostrils filled with the clean citrus scent of him, and her knees went weak.

"I'd better go," she said as she took a step back. "I'm sure you were doing something important since you answered the door without looking to see who was on the other side."

"Just unpacking and…"

"Well, well," a male voice said from behind her. "Am I interrupting something here?"

Damn! He's gay. I should've known that it was too good to be true, she thought as she started to back away. "I'm sorry," she said turning to who she thought was Brent's boyfriend. "This place had been empty for so long, when I heard movement, I just had to come see what was going on. Welcome to the building, I'm Mimi."

"Whoa, I don't live here," he said. "I'm Jamal, by the way."

Mimi smiled. "Nice to meet you. Well, I've done the nosy neighbor thing, so I guess it's time for me to go."

"Don't leave yet, pretty lady," he said. "Me and my boy hang out a lot. Why don't you and some of your equally pretty female friends show us the neighborhood?"

"Jamal," Brent chided. "Leave Ms. Collins alone."

Jamal snapped his fingers. "As in Mimi Collins? Damn, girl, you were all over the news today."

Brent looked from Jamal to Mimi. "The news?"

Mimi fanned her hand. "It was nothing serious. Just…"

Jamal pointed at her. "She writes that blog, the *Misadventures of Mimi.* Women swear by it and you're hard on the brothers, if I must say so myself."

Mimi folded her arms across her chest. "Only those who deserve it. Did I step on your toes, Jamal?"

"Sassy and fine. We should get married," he said with a wink. "You going out tonight? Maybe I can give you some material to write about?"

"You're doing a great job of that right now." Mimi turned to Brent. "It was nice meeting you, Brent." She shot Jamal a salty glance. "The pleasure was all yours." As Mimi walked away, she felt Brent and Jamal watching her. She couldn't help but put a little twist in her hips as she walked to her door. *Life just got a little more interesting.*

Chapter 3

When MJ returned to Mimi's she found her friend sitting on the sofa with her laptop resting on her thighs.

"You're kidding me, right?" she asked.

"I've got to start locking my door," Mimi quipped. She took a look at MJ and shot her a thumbs-up. "Work it, lady. You look great."

MJ smoothed her knee-skimming black leather dress. The spaghetti straps highlighted her toned arms and ample bosom. "This old thing?"

"Whatever. I bet you bought it as soon as your 'client' invited you to the lounge tonight."

"For the last time, we have a professional relationship and that's it. Why aren't you dressed?"

"Do you know who just moved in here?" she asked with a gleam in her eyes.

"Who? The Rock?"

Mimi rolled her eyes. "I need you to get over your obsession with Dwayne Johnson."

"La-la-la, I'm not listening! But can you get dressed already?" MJ said.

"Brent Daniels is my new neighbor."

MJ brought her hand to her mouth. "The lawyer who never loses?"

Mimi nodded and pointed to the picture on her laptop. "This does him no justice. That man is superfine."

"And how do you know this?"

"Because I heard movement in the empty unit, so I went to see what was going on. He answered the door and it was all I could do to keep drool from dripping out of my mouth."

MJ glanced at his picture and shook her head. "That's your type."

Mimi turned her head back to the screen. Brent was milk chocolate with slate-gray eyes, a body built for sin and redemption, and a heart-stopping smile. Okay, that was everything that sent her heart fluttering, but looks only went so far.

Roderick Mason had been a master at teaching that lesson. He'd promised her the fairy tale, but ended up being the frog. Not only had he cheated on Mimi, but he'd stolen her credit card and bought the other woman an engagement ring.

Livid, she'd gone straight to the internet after pressing charges against Roderick for identity theft and told her story of betrayal, with pictures and the police report. Who knew that heartbreak would've given her a new career?

"I'm not saying he isn't fine, but the last thing I'm looking for is a serious relationship," Mimi said. "But I wouldn't mind waking up with him on a Sunday morning."

MJ sucked her teeth. "There you go with that Sunday morning nonsense. You need to wake up and go to church some Sunday morning, instead of deciding that your Saturday night was a mistake."

Mimi laughed, thinking that she hadn't had one of those Saturday nights in a long time. Even though most of her blog posts were about relationships, Mimi had decided that she enjoyed being single. She reveled in her freedom to do whatever she wanted to without questions from anyone.

"Whatever, Mikey. I'm not like you, who has to know a man's Beacon score before you allow him to buy you a drink."

"Shut up and please get dressed."

Mimi glanced at the screen one last time. Brent was nice eye candy, but she was sure that he was one of those men with a phone full of women happy to warm his bed the minute he called. Rising to her feet, Mimi headed to her bedroom to get dressed.

Brent was impressed with the lounge Jamal had chosen. The smooth jazz soothed him as he sat at the bar. "I'm surprised you'd come to a joint like this," Brent said to his friend after they ordered drinks and hot wings.

"Because this is the spot where you meet the women who are classy in the streets and freaks in the sheets."

Brent shook his head. "It's always about chasing women for you, huh?"

Jamal nodded toward a couple of women who were

standing at the entrance of the club. "Those are women worth chasing," Jamal said.

Brent sipped his drink and shook his head. "You're something else. What are you going to do when the right woman comes along?"

"She doesn't exist. So I'm going to buy Miss Right Now a drink." Jamal casually walked over to the entrance and greeted the women he had noticed from the bar. Brent was about to order another drink when he spotted her. Mimi Collins was a vision in gold. Her full lips were painted red and those expressive eyes of her shone in the dim light of the lounge. Her smooth skin looked as if it were carved from mythical wood. The way she wore that knee-skimming strapless gold dress that hugged her curves like a second skin made his body hard as a brick. "Damn," he muttered as he set his drink on the bar. The bartender noticed Brent's stare.

"Brother, you don't stand a chance," he said.

"What are you talking about?"

"If you keep staring at Mimi like that, when she comes over here, she's going to give you hell," he said.

"I wasn't staring… Wait, you know Mimi?"

"Firecracker? Yeah. Went to college with her and Michael."

"Michael? Is that her husband or something?"

He nodded at the woman standing next to Mimi. "Michael, who goes by MJ, is her best friend. She helps me with the marketing for the club." The bartender extended his hand to Brent. "I'm Nicolas Prince, the owner."

Brent shook his hand. "Owner and bartender?"

"A little short-staffed tonight, but I don't mind meeting my clientele. And just a little advice: if Mimi's on

your radar, you better be ready to have your relationship broadcast to hundreds of thousands of readers.
Her blog is popular and she has no filter."

All Brent could think was that didn't seem like the
woman he'd met earlier. Mimi was a bit of a mystery,
but in that dress, he knew he wanted to unravel every
part. Still, her blog gave him pause. He didn't like the
spotlight, and it seemed as if she lived for it, according to Nicolas. When he saw Mimi and MJ heading
toward the bar, he turned back to Nicolas.

"Whatever they're drinking, put it on my tab."

Nicolas gave him a toothy grin. "You don't know
what kind of minefield you just stepped on."

"She can't be that bad."

"Don't believe me, just watch."

And watch Brent did as Mimi and MJ walked over
to the bar. Mimi had the sexiest walk he'd ever seen—
confident and alluring. And those legs. Long and
strong. Immediately, he thought about them wrapped
around his waist while he drove into her wetness.

"Fancy meeting you here," Mimi said, breaking into
his erotic thoughts. "I'd say you're a stalker, but I know
this is a hot spot, thanks to the brilliant woman behind
the marketing."

"I never have to stalk a woman. And I must say, you
look amazing in gold."

She smiled, then turned to Nicolas. "You're the bartender today?"

"Good to see you, too, Mimi," he said while smiling
at MJ. Brent noticed that MJ and Nicolas had started
talking in hushed tones. From the way she was smiling,
whatever he was saying to her must have been good.

Mimi shook her head and reached for the bowl of

peanuts next to Brent. "They get on my nerves," she said, then rolled her eyes.

"That's not nice to say about your friends," he said.

"If only you knew the story. And for the record, I only have one friend over there, and that's MJ." She popped a nut in her mouth and Brent shifted in his seat. Lips like hers were sinful.

"I'd like to know your story. Everyone who knows you has something interesting to say about you."

Mimi smirked and then licked her bottom lip. "So, you've been asking about me? All you had to do was knock on my door. I might have even given you a cup of sugar."

Brent took a quick sip of his drink to cool the heated desire building in his belly. She had to know what that move with her tongue did. She was sexy and owned every bit of it. "I didn't ask. Everything was volunteered, Firecracker."

Mimi tossed a handful of nuts in Nicolas's direction. "Really, Nic?" she snapped when he and MJ turned her way. "You just talking about me to strangers?"

"Mimi, I was trying to save the guy from one of your rants. Warn him that you're nuts," Nic said with a laugh as he brushed peanuts off the bar. MJ touched his shoulder.

"I hope you two aren't going to start acting up this evening," she said. "Tonight is about celebrating." MJ shot Mimi a cautioning look.

Mimi glanced at Brent and held back her caustic comment. "I'm here for the music," she replied.

Nic held up his hands. "Mimi, you know I love you like a sister. An annoying little sister, but I love you nonetheless."

"Whatever," she said, keeping her eyes on Brent, who seemed amused by the scene in front of him.

"I took a look at your blog. It's very popular," Brent said. "A relationship expert, huh?"

"Hardly. I'm a lifestyle blogger. It just so happens that it seems as if people around the world are always interested in bad dating stories."

"So that's why you date, to have stories?"

"Technically, I don't date," she said, then popped a peanut in her mouth. "I go to events, watch people and tell stories about it. What I really want to do is start traveling and be a black girl around the globe, or something like that."

"That sounds good and everything, but is this your career?"

Mimi raised her right eyebrow and shot him a cold look. "I'm sorry that I don't want to spend my time locked behind a desk in a stuffy office with bad lighting. I have the talent to make the world my office. And since you were all over Google checking me out, you see I wrote a bestselling book about dating, so don't try me like that."

"Hey, I didn't mean any harm. Go for it, black girl around the globe."

She rolled her eyes. "Does being condescending win many cases for you?"

"Ouch," he said as he downed his drink. "You speak your mind without hesitation. That's pretty sexy."

"And that was pretty sexist. Insult the woman, then try flirting with her to shut her up."

"Damn, Mimi, you don't give people a chance at all, do you?"

"Those who deserve it," she said. "Pity, I thought

you'd be one of those people. I'm glad we had this talk." She started to stand and Brent touched her elbow.

Mimi tried to pretend that the feel of Brent's hand on her skin didn't affect her. She wanted to act as if their tête-à-tête hadn't been the most interesting conversation she'd had with the opposite sex in a long time. She wanted to muster the strength to storm away from him as she would've done with any other guy who'd pissed her off. But Brent was different. She liked him. Liked that he challenged her and wasn't a pushover.

He just didn't need to know that.

"Please get your hands off me," she said quietly.

"After we dance, I won't ever touch you again," he said with a smile that made her heart skip three beats. Brent stood up and wrapped his arm around Mimi's waist. Without giving her a chance to protest, he ushered her to the dance floor as the band began to play a slow groove.

The moment he pulled her against his chest, Mimi sighed. His arms felt so good. And the man had some moves. His hip thrusts seemed to foretell nights of pleasure wrapped in the bed. Not to be outdone, Mimi unleashed her own moves, spinning and doing a quick step that rivaled the winner of *Dancing with the Stars*. A few other couples around them stopped to watch the sensual movements Mimi and Brent were doing. When the song ended, half of the applause was for Brent and Mimi rather than the band.

"Not bad," he said. "I get the feeling that you have a lot of surprises underneath that gold dress."

She smiled, hoping that her heartbeat would return

to normal as he drank in her image. "Wouldn't you like to know?"

"Right now, I'm just going to buy you a drink," he replied with a smile.

I could wake up Sunday morning with him, she thought as they headed back to the bar.

Chapter 4

By the time Brent and Mimi pushed through the crowd and made it back to the bar, there wasn't an open seat in sight.

"Well, that escalated rather quickly," Mimi quipped. She scanned the crowd for MJ and wasn't surprised when she found her friend in a corner with Nic. "I guess the real bartender showed up."

"If he didn't, that would explain the traffic jam at the bar. I didn't realize there were so many people in here. Then again, with my workload, I don't get to hang out in the Atlanta popular spots much."

Mimi hadn't noticed either, because when she'd been wrapped in Brent's arms nothing else had mattered.

"Want to get out of here?" she asked.

"Sound like a great plan. I'm not fond of big crowds," Brent replied, then draped his arm around Mimi's shoulders as a wave of people pushed passed them. His possessive touch sent a wave of pleasure down her spine. She wiggled out of the intimate embrace because it felt so good.

"Some Waffle House would be really good," Mimi said. "Nic and his tapas menu isn't going to work for me tonight. I'm really hungry." Though her hunger had more to do with the man she'd been dancing with than food.

"Man, I haven't had a pecan waffle and grits in a minute." He glanced at Mimi's svelte figure. "And I see this isn't a habit for you either."

"Two hours a few times a week in the gym while writing makes up for my indulgent foodie ways," she said as they headed for the exit. "But for the record, I hate grits."

"A foodie, huh? Do you ever write about that on your blog?"

"Have you ever read my blog?"

"Not closely. I gave it a glance earlier, remember."

Mimi rolled her eyes. "Rule number one, never tell a blogger that you don't read her blog."

"I prefer to be honest."

She sucked her teeth. "What a tragic character flaw. Wait a minute, you're a lawyer, and you lie every day."

"Wrong. I'm closed on Sundays."

"Aww, so you admit it!"

Brent shook his head. "Admit what?"

She rolled her eyes. "It is too late to play this verbal jujitsu. Let's just go eat and be good neighbors."

"Sounds like a plan," he said. "But I'm a little curious about something."

"What's that?"

"Why do you open your personal life up for the world to see?"

Mimi shrugged. "Because I write about things that women can relate to. I'm doing a public service, you know."

"Interesting way of thinking. Very creative. I guess I'm going to have to subscribe to your blog," he said with a wink. Then Brent glanced down at Mimi's shoes. "Are you sure you're going to be able to make it in those sky-high heels?"

Mimi nodded. "The sidewalk is my runway. Just don't let me fall. And if you like my blog, you should buy my book, too."

Brent laughed. "I will definitely catch you and buy your book if you promise to sign it."

The short walk to the Waffle House did prove to be a little bit of torture, but not because of Mimi's shoes. It was Brent. Every time she took a breath, his masculine scent filled her nostrils and sent waves of desire through her body. She couldn't figure out if it was sandalwood or just his natural scent that was driving her crazy.

As they walked into the restaurant, Brent placed his hand on the small of her back and an electric jolt rushed through her body. *Be still my beating heart,* she thought.

"Booth or the counter?" he asked.

"Booth, for sure." She glanced at the people standing at the counter waiting for take-out orders. "It's too busy over there."

Brent nodded in agreement and they took a seat at a table in the back of the restaurant. Mimi nervously grabbed the plastic menu and pretended to study it, while she quietly checked Brent out. He looked really good with clothes on. His tailored shirt hugged the muscles she'd seen up close.

"I thought you knew what you wanted," Brent said. "You're studying that menu as if it's an SAT exam."

Mimi lowered the menu and smirked at him. "I took the ACT and made a perfect score. I'm just thinking about trying something new." *Like you.*

"Can't go wrong with a pecan waffle," he said. "And bacon."

"Not a fan of pork," she said. "But I think a pecan waffle and cheese eggs are just what I need."

What she really felt like she needed was his lips pressed against hers, his tongue dancing with hers as they stripped each other naked. Biting her full bottom lip, Mimi wondered what would be the consequences of sleeping with her neighbor. Yes, she'd have to see him again. There would be that awkward moment after she dipped out of his place and went home. And suppose he brought someone home? Would she go all deranged ex or mind her business? Guess that would depend on how good the sex was.

A waitress walked over to the table to take Mimi's and Brent's orders. After they told her what they wanted and she walked away, Brent focused on Mimi and smiled.

"So," he began. "Why do people call you *firecracker*?"

Mimi rolled her eyes. "Nic calls me that because he can't handle a woman who doesn't fawn all over him, like MJ. And people don't call me that."

Brent leaned back in the booth. "I think it fits."

"You don't even know me like that."

"Let's see, you—by your own admission—are nosy. You speak your mind and I get the feeling that you can be rather explosive."

Mimi raised her right eyebrow at him. "And you've figured all of this out from knowing me less than twelve hours?" She looked down at her watch for effect.

"Part of the job. I have to be a good judge of character." Brent smiled again and her heart fluttered.

Get it together, girl, she chided herself.

Mimi rolled her eyes again and held her tongue, lest he make another judgment about her. "Anyway, Matlock," she said, "you've asked a lot of questions tonight and shared nothing about yourself."

"I'm sure you ran a Google search," he replied with a wink.

"Like you didn't do the same thing. You're a heavy hitter in the legal community and you give back to Big Brothers Big Sisters. Google makes you seem like you're all work and no play. A little staid."

Brent nodded. "I don't know if I should be impressed or insulted."

"Why are you hiding behind all of your good press? Angry exes? You're really a playboy like your friend, Jamal?"

"Why do you immediately go for the negative?"

She shrugged. "Because no one is perfect and I like to know what I'm dealing with up front."

"Who hurt you?"

Mimi was about reply when the waitress returned with their coffee and iced tea. After Brent watched her pour sugar and creamer into her steaming cup of coffee, he asked, "Well?"

"Well what?"

"You're guarded and I'm sure there is a reason."

She took a long, slow sip of her coffee. "And," she said after swallowing, "you think I'm just going to open up to you because you have pretty eyes?" *Why did I say that? Now he's going to think I'm flirting.*

"Usually works on beautiful women, but I see Mimi Collins is a different breed," he quipped. "Can I ask one last question?"

"You can ask, but I'm not going to promise that I'll answer."

"Is Mimi your real name or your pen name?"

"Nickname. My government name is Mariah."

"Beautiful name. It fits you." Brent smiled at her and took a sip of his tea. Mimi's cheeks heated under his stare. It felt as if Brent saw through all of her walls, and that never happened.

"Maybe if I were a singer and had bigger boobs," she said. Mimi rolled her eyes and silently chided herself. She'd written about women doing the same brainless thing she was doing right now. Wasn't she the one who wrote about men being hunters and women shouldn't make themselves seem too available?

"Funny," he said. "I think everything about you is just fine."

Sighing, Mimi figured that since she'd made every mistake that she warned her readers about, she might as well go for the gusto.

"Why are you still single?" she asked. "You're everything that women in Atlanta want. You should have a girlfriend, fiancée, wife or at least a baby mama."

"I never said I was single," Brent said.

Mimi's eyes widened. "Oh, so…"

"My career is my everything right now. Too many

women say I make them feel like a mistress because work comes first."

"There's nothing wrong with that. You don't reach your level of success without hard work and sacrifice."

"Easy to say when you aren't dating me and I'm working on a case that keeps me out very late."

"You have a point there," she said. "But the solution is don't date. It's too stressful and when it stops being fun, you should always move on."

"Wow, that's not even how it's supposed to work."

"It works for me. Besides, you can't say that you're looking for the white picket fence, two point five kids and a fluffy dog."

Brent sipped his tea, then nodded. "That's exactly what I'm looking for. I just haven't found the right woman to share my vision."

"When you build that time machine and head back to the 1950s, invite me to the wedding. I love wedding cake. Never tasted a piece of dry wedding cake."

Brent laughed and Mimi closed her eyes. The sound of his laughter sent tingles down her spine that settled between her thighs. And as much as she wanted to blame it on the alcohol, she couldn't because she'd had one weak drink at the bar. She wanted this man. Wanted his touch and to feel those lips against hers. Sure, her body was a little love-starved. But she had to pull herself together. Since this man was her neighbor, she knew that they could never be anything but friends. And that could be fun, she told herself as the waitress brought their food over.

The scent of the breakfast fare made Mimi's mouth water for another reason. She was actually hungry for food. Mimi struggled to take dainty bites of her food, even though she was starving.

As she watched syrup drip from her waffle, Mimi decided that her charade had gone on long enough. She wasn't on a date and she wasn't going to pretend that she wasn't starving.

Brent was mesmerized by Mimi's mouth. Her full lips closed around the fork and he couldn't tear his eyes away when she licked her lips when the syrup dripped down from the utensil. When their eyes met as she spooned eggs into her mouth, she raised her eyebrow.

Swallowing, she asked, "What?"

"Nothing," he replied with a smirk.

Mimi dropped her fork and wiped her mouth. "So, the way I eat must have ruled me out as your 1950s ideal woman." She shrugged and laughed. "I'm okay with that."

"You're funny. I think this is the beginning of a beautiful friendship. One question, do you like football?"

She scrunched up her nose. "Not really. But I'm a season ticket holder for the Atlanta Hawks because of something I wrote in my book."

"Yeah, I really need to become your best friend fast."

"That could happen. How handy are you with hanging flat-screen televisions?"

"There's not much I can't do with my hands," he bragged. Mimi nibbled on her bottom lip and Brent wondered what her lips would feel like pressed against his.

"When are you going to prove all of this to me?"

she asked. "I mean, I just bought a television for my bedroom."

Brent looked down at his watch. Yes, it was too late to roll into someone's bedroom, especially someone who looked like Mimi.

"In the morning," he said.

"Technically, it is morning. I wanted to hook up my PlayStation and see what this new game that's on everybody's lips is all about."

"You're a gamer, too? Mimi, why are you still single? If you read comics, you're a nerd's dream woman."

She folded her arms across her chest as if she were offended. "Really? Who said I wanted to be anyone's dream woman, particularly a nerd?"

"We're the new dream men," Brent said, laughing.

"I'm not getting the nerd vibe from you," she said. "So, are you going to hook up my TV or not?"

"Why not?" he said. "Let's just hope we don't start a scandal in the complex."

Mimi laughed. "Really? I'm sure we're not being watched yet."

"Oh, yeah, that's right. I'm going into the nosy neighbor's spot."

She reached across the table and pinched him on the arm. "Whatever, nerd. Superman or Batman?"

"Black Panther. I'm a Marvel Comics guy. But if I had to choose, I'd go with Batman. Superman is just too perfect. Who can live up to that?"

Mimi narrowed her eyes at him. "But he's all about truth, justice and the American way. How can a lawyer not believe in that?"

"But he isn't even American. Batman knows the truth."

Mimi couldn't really argue with that. "Still, everyone loves Superman."

"And I guess that's what you're looking for, Superman?"

"No way. I could never share my man with the world and be all right with that."

Brent laughed and then took a spoonful of grits into his mouth. Mimi was something else. And he was definitely intrigued.

They finished eating, falling into easy conversation, and he decided that they definitely liked each other.

Chapter 5

Mimi's walk had changed to a shuffle as they left the Waffle House.

"Come here," Brent said as they stopped in front of a bench near a MARTA stop.

"Why?" She sighed as she tried to ignore the throbbing in her toes. Her shoes had officially reached their time limit. Brent tugged at her arm until she joined him on the bench.

"We've already decided that we don't have to impress each other. Give me the shoes," he said.

"Umm, why?"

"Girl, you know your feet hurt. Give me the shoes."

Mimi took her heels off and handed them over. Then Brent took her left foot into his hands, slowly kneading and massaging her insole. Mimi struggled not to moan in delight. So, he was good—no, amazing—with his hands. By the time he switched to her right foot, Mimi was ready to buy him a lifetime supply of bacon and bourbon.

"Oh my goodness," she exclaimed. "I believe that was all the proof I needed about you and your hands. I think I could run a marathon in those shoes now."

"How did you get to the lounge tonight?" he asked.

"I rode with MJ." Mimi reached into her handbag to retrieve her phone. She wasn't surprised that she didn't have a single text or missed call from her friend. Mimi knew that she was in Nic-land and nothing else really mattered right now.

"It's not that far of a walk back to our place. Jamal just sent me a message. He's going to be otherwise occupied for the rest of the night."

"You know, our friends are kind of selfish," Mimi quipped, then she held her hand out. "My shoes, please."

"Why would you want to put those skyscrapers on again?"

"Because I'm not walking on this dirty ground in my bare feet," she said matter-of-factly.

"Then there's only one solution," he said, then scooped her up in his arms. Mimi would've protested, called him sexist or an ogre, if the heat from his body didn't feel so good.

"You're sure you can carry all of this home?" Then she pointed to her shoes beside the MARTA bench. "And you can *not* leave my shoes!"

Sitting her on the bench, he picked up the shoes and handed them to her. And as if he could read her mind, he picked her up again before she could put them on.

"Oh, you don't trust me?" she asked with a laugh.

"Your eyes tell everything. I saw you looking at those killer heels and I knew your next move."

Mimi leaned her head against his chest as they walked. "What are you into? CrossFit, power lifting?"

"Actually, yoga," he said. "Nothing helps me unwind after a stressful case like the sun salutation. And then there's boxing."

"Aww, I get it, peace and violence. That's interesting," she said, then took a deep breath. There was that scent again. Definitely sandalwood. Definitely driving her crazy.

"Sometimes it takes more than the downward facing dog to get you to sleep."

Mimi raised her right eyebrow at him. "I'm just going to keep my mouth shut," she said, then shook her head.

"What? You said you spend a lot of time at the gym. You know a sweaty workout can be better than sex with the wrong person."

"Well… You do have a point. But let's be real, you have a lot of women to choose from, you just don't. Makes you seem as if you're the good guy."

"How do you figure that? Just because I'm the finest man you've come across in a while, it doesn't mean that I use all this sexy for evil."

"Jamal is sexier," she quipped.

"I'd drop you if I knew you weren't telling the biggest lie in Atlanta," he said as they turned onto the block where their complex was.

"I know Jamal has more interaction with the ladies. I saw his work tonight. I can't believe sisters still fall for that mess."

"What mess is that? Maybe I need to add it to my repertoire."

She rolled her eyes. "How about, I'll tell you after you hang my TV, Mr. Good Hands?"

"If you don't tell me, I'm not hanging the TV," he said with a wink.

"That's just dirty."

"All right, here's a compromise: you tell me while I hang it."

"Okay, that works. And you can put me down now."

Brent pressed the code to enter the building, but didn't put Mimi down. "This isn't much cleaner than the sidewalk near the MARTA station," he said. "When we get inside, I'll let you go."

Mimi sighed. Something about him letting her go made her feel some kind of way. But she told herself that they were just going to be friends and she shouldn't get comfortable in his arms. But she knew it was too late for that.

When he lowered her to the floor, they headed for the elevator. "What made you move into this area?" she asked.

"Closer to the office, no more fighting two-eight-five traffic every morning."

"Maybe you can show me your office one day."

"It would probably bore you."

She nodded. "You might be right. I bore easily. That's why I don't work in an office."

"Have you ever?"

"Worst two years of my life. I was a stringer for a paper and they offered me a position to create their blog. I thought I was going to be out creating content and making it pop. It was all about monitoring the page views and watching other people have fun. I told them that I wanted to have a more creative role on my blog. They said no. I started my own blog and they didn't like it, so I was fired."

"Damn."

Mimi shrugged. "I could've begged for my job back, but I was like, why not work for someone you really like? I took it as a sign that I needed to work for myself."

"Interesting," he said. "Were you at all nervous that it wouldn't work out?"

She nodded. "But if it didn't at least I could say that I tried. Thank goodness it did work." They walked to Mimi's door in silence. Then she turned to him. "You seem as if you pretty much follow the rules all the time," she said when she unlocked the front door.

"Well, that's normally what good lawyers do."

"All that time in law school to be a part of the status quo." Mimi shook her head as she tossed her shoes inside, then turned the light on.

Mimi watched Brent as he gazed around the living room, taking in the eclectic art and vibrant colors.

"What's with the one red wall?" he asked.

"That's where I do my vlogs. Red is also the background color of my logo," she said.

"So this is the home office?"

"I guess. I'd like to not think of it as an office, though. Anyway, you can have a tour after you hang my TV."

"And you can tell me about your observations tonight."

"If you must know, the average woman wants her ego stroked just like a man. It's just when y'all do it, you have to seem sincere or it comes off creepy. Jamal was brilliant at it. I'm sure when the sister he wakes up with in the morning decides to cook him breakfast, she isn't going to realize that she'll never see him again."

"And what crystal ball do you see all of this in?"

Mimi crossed the room and booted up her desktop computer. Then she pulled up her blog site and pointed to Brent. "Please get familiar with my crystal ball," she said.

Brent crossed over to her computer and glanced at the website. "This is funny," he said. "But why would you go to an event like this if you weren't looking for Mr. Right?"

"Well, I was invited and it turned out to be false advertising. Remember, I'm also doing a public service. It's a shame how companies prey on the fact that so many women are looking for love and marriage. I wrote a book about how hard it is to date in Atlanta and then here comes this company that's promising true love to women, but cheap sex to men. I wouldn't have been doing my job if I'd allowed this to go without reporting on it."

"And you're not one of those women who's looking for Mr. Right?"

"No. That's overrated. If marriage is the ultimate goal, you're only setting yourself up for failure."

"Cynical much?" he asked.

"Not cynical, just realistic. Anyway, it's time for you to put your hands to use," she said as she smiled at him.

"Lead the way," he said. Mimi started for the stairs.

"Just keep in mind that the TV is all you're touching tonight," she said as she looked over her shoulder at him.

"There's always tomorrow," he said with a smirk.

Mimi turned her head and closed her eyes. If only he knew.

When Brent followed Mimi into her bedroom, she had to silently remind herself that they weren't going to fall into bed. But her eyes fell to her rose-colored blanket and green duvet. She wouldn't mind him laying her down on the soft covers and making love to her.

Stop it, she thought as she crossed over to her walk-in closet and pulled out the TV box.

"Let me get that," Brent said from behind her. The deep timbre of his voice sent shivers up her spine. Mimi stepped aside and watched Brent lift the TV as if it weighed three ounces. Underneath his tailored shirt, she could see his bulging muscles.

"Where do you want it?" he asked as he glanced around the room.

Mimi pointed to the wall facing her bed. "I had Manny check and make sure I could drill the bracket in place."

"Who's Manny?"

"Oh, you haven't met Manny yet? He's the building super. And if you want something done right, you don't call him."

"Then how do you know he was right about the wall?"

Mimi shrugged. "I guess if you don't get electrocuted we'll know."

"That's cold," he said. "You lured me up here to risk my life so that you can play Xbox."

"PlayStation," she corrected. "And if I remember correctly, you came willingly."

Brent walked over to the wall and drummed on it. "Doesn't seem as if there's anything back here that will kill me. Mimi, where are your tools?"

"Under the bed," she said, then dropped to her knees.

Brent couldn't take his eyes off Mimi's shapely behind as she crawled underneath her bed. She moved with the grace of a panther and when she stretched forward, he got hard. His body reacted in a way that he hadn't expected. When was the last time that a woman gave him this feeling? Not since he was a teenager. As a grown man, he was supposed to be able to control his emotions and body, not act like a youngster looking at his first copy of *Playboy.* But damn! As she inched deeper underneath the bed and wiggled her ass, it took every ounce of self-control in him to stop from mounting Mimi from behind.

"All right," she said as she slammed the tools on the edge of the bed. "Here's my toolbox."

Mimi was a goddess, Brent decided as he drank in the image of her tousled hair and full lips. When she flicked her tongue across her bottom lip, he nearly lost it.

"Would you like something to drink?" she asked.

"Sounds good," he said, then unbuttoned his shirt.

"Cranberry juice works for you?" she asked as she turned away from his shirtless frame.

"Yes."

She released a sigh as she took a quick look at him and then headed out the door.

Chapter 6

Mimi gulped down a cold cup of cranberry juice. She thought about adding vodka to the cup, but figured it was a bad idea. Her body was on fire and she had a notion to run up to her bedroom and wrap herself around Brent.

Another sip of juice. She'd have to get naked first. Mimi looked down at her dress and gasped. Did she really crawl under the bed in this? Was her bra really exposed?

Final sip. She knew she needed to be sober. Mimi adjusted her dress and poured two glasses of juice and turned toward the stairs. She took two steps and stopped. What if she made a fool of herself and acted on her carnal thoughts? *You're better than this. Brent is installing a TV. He already told you he wants a family-minded woman to fall for and you're more than a*

*booty call. That would be a great blog post. Oh my
goodness, I'm losing my mind here.*

Mimi slowly walked upstairs and reminded herself
to keep her hands off Brent. When she saw him with
his hands raised above his head, she almost dropped
the juice.

"I thought you'd forgotten about me up here slav-
ing for your right to play games." Brent shook his head
and laughed.

"How could I forget that you're in my bedroom?"
she asked as she extended a glass of cranberry juice.
Half naked and looking like you should be in my bed?

"Thank you."

She smiled. "No problem."

"Ooh, that was good." Brent said, then handed the
empty glass to Mimi. "Let me plug this in and make
sure I did it right." He bent over and Mimi downed her
cold juice to quell the fire burning inside her belly as
she had a flash of Brent taking his pants off and crawl-
ing into bed with her.

"Mimi," he said. "Are you all right?"

"What? Yeah."

"Did you hear what I said?"

She hadn't even realized that he'd turned to face
her. "No, I didn't."

"Where's your remote and that PlayStation you can't
wait to play?"

She fanned her hand at him. She wanted to play a
different kind of game and that couldn't happen. "I'll
hook that up tomorrow. You did all the heavy lifting.
I'm good now."

"All right, then I'm going to head home," he said

as he picked his shirt up from the floor. "Mimi, it's been a pleasure."

She blushed as he headed out of her bedroom. Too bad he was one of those men who wanted serious. She didn't do serious. Not anymore. *Once bitten, twice shy,* she thought as she followed him downstairs.

Alone in his home, Brent couldn't sleep. Mimi filled his mind. Her hips. Her lips. That come-hither look in her eyes when she looked at him. Jamal would've woken up with Mimi—or at least tried. But Brent knew a woman like Mimi could be nothing but trouble. Fun, but trouble.

Sitting up in his king-size bed, Brent squeezed the bridge of his nose. He'd spent his adult life avoiding trouble and crafting an image that could handle all of the scrutiny being Brent Daniels Jr. caused.

When he'd been in law school, his father—also a lawyer—made the Daniels name infamous when he represented a Mafia hit man in a high-profile murder case. To get his client a favorable sentence, Brent Daniels Sr. attempted to blackmail the judge. When that didn't work, the judge's family had been threatened.

The judge had reported the blackmail attempt and the death threats to the FBI, and Brent Sr. had been arrested, tried and sentenced to twenty-five years in prison. The media had held on to the story about the disgraced attorney like a dog with a meaty ham bone. The details of the story played on the evening news and ran across the front page of local and regional newspapers. Brent left Georgia to finish law school at Tulane in New Orleans. When he'd graduated at the top of his class, his father's sins came back to haunt him, follow him and make getting a job in Louisiana impossible. So he'd spent the first five years of his career in New York. He'd made such a name for himself that when he decided to move back to Atlanta and open his firm, people knew there was a stark difference between Sr. and Jr.

In the five years that he'd been in business in Atlanta, Brent had put nineteen young men through Morehouse with his Martha Joyce Daniels scholarship. He named it after his late grandmother after his mother, Yancy Williams, told him she wanted nothing to do with publicity since she'd gone back to using her maiden name.

Brent wanted to restore some sort of pride to his family name and make sure no one ever confused him and his father. These days, questions about his father only came up around the anniversary of his conviction. Since he'd been sentenced to federal prison, he would never be paroled.

Brent hadn't seen his father since he'd been a teenager, and their last meeting ended with Brent Sr. telling him that he'd never amount to anything because his mother made him soft.

That accusation made Brent work harder than ever. And his success was the greatest way to try to erase the stain on his family name. That's why he made sure every move he made wasn't a media moment. Mimi was obviously a media firestorm. Hell, she'd spent the day all over the news.

He needed to stay away from her, but knowing that she was just across the hall, that was going to be harder than his erection.

Brent was in trouble, but he wasn't upset about it.

* * *

Mimi jolted awake in her bed, half expecting to see Brent there. When she felt the pillow, she was a bit disappointed. She'd spent the night dreaming of his arms wrapped around her as he thrust in and out of her wetness. Looking down at her thighs, she was reminded of how they trembled in her dream as he licked and sucked her core.

"Stop it," she muttered, then swung her legs over the side of the bed. Mimi knew she had work to do, and wallowing in fantasyland wasn't the move for the day.

But first, she had to burn off some energy with a run. Mimi grabbed her workout gear and cell phone, then headed downstairs to mix a protein shake. As she looked out over the city, she felt that urge to leave again.

Mimi tried to pretend that she didn't want the love she wrote about. Tried to pretend that it didn't matter, but she did want to fall in love. She wanted a marriage like her mother and father—Adrienne and Melvin Collins—but she'd kissed too many frogs to believe that she'd ever find Prince Charming. They didn't make men like her dad anymore. What her parents had was special, and her generation of men didn't want special. They wanted robots with the perfect ass and cooking skills like Bobby Flay, while they offered nothing but lip service, in her opinion.

Mimi knew her parents' fifty-year relationship wasn't something she could have. Especially in image-conscious Atlanta. She didn't have a high-powered job; she was artsy and a free spirit, something her dad said she got from her grandmother. Her mother encouraged her to think outside the box and do what made her happy. Writing and her blog gave her joy. Unfortunately, her happiness never landed her the love she craved.

These days, she wasn't content. Wasn't feeling creative or as if she was going to further her career just sitting in her comfort zone in Atlanta. She wanted to have some real adventures and do something exciting. The world was calling her and there was nothing to stop her from answering.

Well, maybe something could be brewing with Brent. Mimi pulled her T-shirt on and took a sip of her protein shake. "Get over yourself," she whispered as she dumped the remainder of her shake in the sink. Heading for the front door, Mimi paused to put her purple running shoes on, then opened the door. The moment she saw Brent walk out of his place she ducked back inside.

From her peephole, she watched him pick up his newspaper from his doorstep. Mimi drank in those bare chocolate arms, the way his silky pajama pants clung to his narrow hips. She couldn't help but wonder if he wore boxers, briefs or nothing at all underneath those pants.

When Brent looked up, Mimi could've sworn that he looked directly at her. Those eyes were penetrating and shook her. She turned away as he closed the door. This was going to be hard.

Mimi opened her door and headed for the elevator. She was probably going to need a six-mile run this morning to clear her mind.

Brent crossed over to his breakfast nook and dropped his newspaper on the granite counter. He had to get

Mimi off his brain, but the glimpse of her he caught awakened his libido more than he expected.

Why did she act like a deer in headlights when she locked eyes with him? *Must be the artist thing. I can't let this woman get under my skin,* he thought as he loaded his coffeemaker with fragrant Kona grounds.

Before he could read his copy of *USA TODAY,* Brent's cell phone rang. When he saw Jamal's name on the caller ID, he started to ignore it. But he answered the call.

"Man," Brent said, "I'm glad I moved to midtown otherwise I'd still be waiting in that bar!"

"Don't even act like that. I saw you and Mimi leave together. You thought I missed that. What time did you send her home?"

"Mimi didn't come over here. I went to her place."

"Damn, you move fast. Did you have a good time?"

"You have a one-track mind. I hope you have a good lawyer on retainer for the epic sexual harassment lawsuit that's going to fall on you one day."

"Why do you think we're friends? Anyway, I know how to act in the workplace. You know that. So, you want some breakfast or are you about to get some with Mimi?"

"There you go assuming. I don't think of every woman as a conquest."

"Nah, just the ones with the right image. You need to stop that and have some fun instead of trying to…"

"Don't start this shit right now. It's too early," Brent groaned.

"All right, let's just get some food and leave this heavy stuff for another day. But I do have one question," Jamal said.

"What?"

"Are you ever going to go see him?"

"Hell no. That man destroyed my family, damn near ruined my career before it started. I don't want to see him."

"But you know…"

"I don't give a damn. Look, I'm going to cool out and get some work done." Brent ended the call. He didn't care that his father was dying; what he did care about was Jamal trying to force this family reunion on him. And why was his friend keeping up with his father's health and well-being?

It really wasn't any of his business how Brent and his father got along. What about his mother, who'd sequestered herself away in South Carolina because she couldn't take the shame of what his father did?

Cancer. That's what was killing him. Brent tried to care, tried to muster up enough emotions to drive to the prison where his father would more than likely die.

Growing up, Brent Sr. had been his hero, his disciplinarian and the man who'd taught him to be an honest man. All that was shattered, and it would never be repaired in Brent's mind.

How could his role model fall hard like that? Brent shook his head, mad that there was still a child inside him missing his father.

In the third mile of her run, Mimi found herself standing in front of MJ's town house. The only thing that stopped her from knocking on the front door was the car in the driveway.

Nic was here. Part of her was happy that her friend had finally admitted how deeply she loved him and they'd sealed the deal. Still, she needed her friend! But there was no way that she would just go bang on the door.

She wondered what her mother would say about her current situation. Would she encourage her to move away and start over or stay in Atlanta and continue the success she was having here?

And then there was Brent. Something sparked between them, but Mimi wasn't going to base her future on a maybe. Maybe they would fall in love, maybe they would like each other beyond Sunday morning. She turned her walk into a slow jog. Then as she thought about shirtless Brent and where she wanted him to touch her, she burst into a full-out sprint.

By the time she made it home, Mimi was a sweaty mess. And of course, Brent was the first face she saw.

"Good run?" he asked.

"Amazing," she said.

"Maybe we should run together one morning. You look like you go very hard." He gave her a slow once-over that heated her more than her run.

"I had some great motivation this morning," she said with a smirk.

"Putting in work so that you won't feel guilty about what you're going to do later?"

Mimi furrowed her brows. "And what is that supposed to mean?"

"Lying in bed playing PlayStation all day. You can't burn a lot of calories that way."

"No, I have creative ways to burn calories in bed," she said, then pushed her damp hair off her forehead.

Brent gave her a cool glance.

"Did you hear me?" she asked. "Earth to Brent, where did you go?"

"You wouldn't want to know."

She rolled her eyes. "I'm going to take a shower. It was good seeing you again."

"You too, Mimi. Hey," he called out as she turned to head inside. "Would you like to join me for dinner?"

Dinner and dessert, she thought. "Sorry, I have plans," she replied, remembering one of her Mimi rules of dating. Never accept a date that could turn into a one-night stand. She told herself to add, *especially with your neighbor.*

"Some other time, then?" he pressed.

Mimi smiled and waved at him before dashing inside. Once she was safely behind closed doors, Mimi took a cleansing breath. Maybe she should've said yes to dinner. They could've gone to a public place and then… They would've had to come to the same place at the end of the night.

"I did the right thing," she muttered as she grabbed a bottle of water and gulped it down. Mimi stripped out of her wet T-shirt and padded toward the stairs. Then there was a knock at her door. Part of her hoped that it was Brent, because she would change her mind and say yes to dinner.

When she saw it was MJ, she couldn't hide her disappointment. Snatching the door open, she pointed her finger at MJ's nose. "Someone has been a bad girl!"

"What are you talking about and why are you half-naked?"

"Went running this morning," she said as they walked into the living room. "Needed to find out why my best friend abandoned me last night…"

"You left me first!"

"I may have left the spot first, but you and Nic disappeared as soon as the music started and the bartender arrived. So, was it worth the wait?"

"What? Huh?"

"My run. I ran to your house and who was parked in the driveway?" Mimi wiggled her eyebrows. "I hope you two know what you're doing this time."

"We're not doing anything. He had a little... I'm hopeless when it comes to that man. Mimi, I love Nic so much and I know he doesn't want a relationship, but when I'm with him, I see wedding dresses and doves."

Mimi shook her head trying to keep her comments to herself, but she knew her friend was cruising for a heartbreak. One of her own causing. Nic made it clear that he wasn't looking for the relationship MJ wanted and deserved.

"You know what," Mimi said. "I know someone you should meet." Since she didn't believe she and Brent had potential for a relationship, Mimi wanted to see MJ happy with a good guy like Brent.

"Umm, now you're Miss Fast Love?"

"No, but can you believe I know a really sexy guy who's just as corny about love as you are? Let me take a shower and then I'll give you the details." Dashing upstairs, she ignored MJ's questions.

Chapter 7

MJ and Mimi headed across the hall, and MJ kept pulling her friend's arm.

"I'm going to freaking kill you," MJ gritted out as Mimi knocked on Brent's door. "What are you doing?"

Mimi turned to MJ. "A big favor for you."

When the door opened, Jamal was standing there with a big grin on his face. "Ladies, did you come to borrow a cup of sugar?"

Mimi rolled her eyes. "Is Brent here?"

"Brent," Jamal barked. "Two beautiful women are at the door for you. Come on in, ladies."

"Who is this clown?" MJ asked. "I know he better not..."

"Shh," Mimi whispered as Brent walked into the living room. She drank in his smooth brown skin covered by a green-and-white Tulane School of Law T-shirt. *Too sexy for words,* she thought when they locked eyes.

"Hey, Mimi. To what do I owe this pleasure?" His smile was so disarming and erotic.

"My friend MJ and I were going to cook some dinner and I wanted to invite you over."

"I thought you had plans," he said as he folded his massive arms across his chest.

"They fell through," she said with a shoulder shrug. "So, do you want to join us or what?"

"What about me?" Jamal asked. "I mean, I'm hungry, too."

Mimi rolled her eyes. "Sorry, we only have enough sushi for three."

"Sushi?" Jamal said. "I don't eat raw fish. Let's have a fish fry instead."

"Nobody invited you!" Mimi said. "And I'm not going to spend the next three days airing the smell of fried fish out of my house!"

"I have an idea," Brent said. "You bring the fish and wine over here and I'll suffer the smell of fish."

"And I get to stay," Jamal said. "Besides, I make some mean hush puppies."

Mimi rolled her eyes. Then an idea popped in her head. "Okay, Brent, why don't you and MJ go pick up the fish and I'll go home and get the wine."

Brent furrowed his brow. What was going on here? "MJ, are you all right with that?"

"No," she said, then smirked at Mimi. "Mimi's the cook, not me. So I'll get the wine and be here when you two return."

Mimi narrowed her eyes at her friend. This wasn't the plan and she was going to get MJ when they were alone.

"Fine," she said. "Let me get my purse. Come on, MJ."

* * *

When Brent and Jamal were alone, they exchanged confused looks. "What just happened here?" Jamal asked.

"I have no idea."

"That MJ girl is fine."

"And I feel like Mimi is trying to hook us up," Brent said.

"Why would she do that when it is so obvious that you two want to get naked, jump into bed and pretend you're married?"

"What are you talking about?" Brent asked.

"Even a blind man can see what's going on with you two." Jamal laughed. "Why do you think she wants her friend to hook up with you? It's clear she wants me."

Brent shook his head. He loved Jamal, but sometimes he could be very delusional. Now was certainly one of those times. He had been surprised to see Jamal at his door after the conversation they'd had that morning, but like the brothers they were, everything had been forgiven and they were going to catch the Braves game before Mimi and MJ showed up.

"I guess living in this building is going to be different," Brent said as there was a knock at the door.

"Better than living in the boondocks," Jamal said as he watched Brent open the door.

Mimi smiled and walked inside without MJ. "Ready to head out?" she asked.

"Where's MJ?" Brent asked.

"Looking for the perfect bottle of wine. I told her Moscato doesn't pair well with fish and hush puppies."

"I guess we'd better get going," Brent said.

"Hey," Jamal said, throwing his hands up. "What about me?"

Mimi rolled her eyes. "I'm the one making the hush puppies, so I know what ingredients to get," he said.

"Fine, I guess we'll make this a nice little three-some," Mimi said. Jamal grinned at Mimi.

"Now you're speaking my language, little mama."

She gritted her teeth. "You know what, I'm going to write a blog about you, Jamal."

"I'm honored."

"Man, shut up," Brent said as they headed out the door.

Brent and Jamal headed toward the parking garage and Mimi shook her head. "Publix is three blocks over. Y'all can't be that lazy."

"No, but I'm sure you don't carry bags," Jamal said.

"We can walk and we'll carry the bags," Brent said as he crossed over to Mimi. She was gorgeous standing there with the sun beaming down on her. Her cinnamon-brown curls were pulled up in a messy bun that highlighted her long neck and beautiful face. Especially those eyes. Brent found himself wanting to get lost in her stare as they made love.

"What?" Mimi asked when she locked eyes with Brent.

"You tell me. I ask you out and then you show up at my door with your friend as if we're in college and you're playing Cupid."

"I'm not… You and MJ have a lot in common. I thought you two should meet. What happens next, hey, y'all are grown."

Brent shook his head. "I don't do blind dates and

I get the feeling that MJ doesn't, either. Nice one, though," he said with a grin.

Mimi brushed her hand across her forehead. She was hot but it had nothing to do with the heat from the Georgia sun and everything to do with Brent and his captivating smile. Nervously licking her lips, Mimi tore her eyes away from him.

"Let's go, guys," she said. Jamal shook his head as he looked at Brent and Mimi walking together like two lovers.

Once they made it to Publix, Mimi's heartbeat had calmed to a normal pace by teasing Jamal and ignoring the heated looks Brent kept showering on her. As it turned out, Jamal wasn't a horrible person. The former marine would be a cool guy if he used his brain more than he used the other head. Then again, he had a point about having fun and enjoying life after seeing so much death in the war.

"Mimi," Brent said as she stood in front of the seafood counter. The sound of his deep voice sent chills down her spine. Turning around, she faced him and tried to be unaffected. She failed.

"Yes?" she asked breathlessly.

"I'm allergic to shrimp," he said. Looking down at her hands, Mimi realized that she'd picked up a bag of shrimp.

"Oh, I'm sorry. Are you allergic to all shellfish? There's a sale on crab legs and lobster tails."

"Just shrimp. I love lobster, but I can do without the crab legs."

Mimi returned the shrimp to the cooler and grabbed four lobster tails. "How do you like it?"

"What?"

"The lobster, how do you like it? Dripping with butter or seasoned?"

The way she said *dripping* made his body throb with desire. He would love to see her dripping with sweat after making love to her all night. "Butter and lemon, that's my thing," he said.

"Typical," she said with a smirk. "I make a mean lobster seasoning that will blow your mind."

"I bet there are a lot of mind-blowing things about you, Mimi," he replied.

Her mouth dropped and she stared at him without saying a word. A rare moment for the ever-outspoken Mimi Collins. "I guess I'm making you uncomfortable," he said after another silent beat passed.

"No, it's just… Brent, I could see myself liking you a whole lot and that's dangerous."

"Why?"

"Because we don't want the same thing," she said, then sighed. "You want the white picket fence. I want to travel and have adventures."

"Whoa, you're putting a wedding before a relationship. I thought you warned women about that on your blog."

She nodded, a little surprised that he had become a regular reader of her blog. "But I see myself wanting something more with you and I'm going to have to stop myself from getting hurt."

"That doesn't sound like a life worth living. I tell you what, let's just be friends and you can stop trying to pawn your girl off on me. I'll control myself the next time I pass a jewelry store."

"What?"

"I won't go in and buy you a three-carat engagement ring."

"Aww, you don't know me at all. I want four carats," she said with a laugh. By the time they headed over to the spice aisle, Mimi felt as if she made a great friend.

Loaded with grocery bags and beer, Jamal, Brent and Mimi started back to the complex. "I knew this was going to happen," Jamal groaned as he hoisted a twelve-pack of beer on his shoulder. "We bought all of this sh…"

"You wanted beer," Mimi pointed out, then held up her two bags. "And I'm carrying something."

"Yeah, salad," he grunted.

"Shut up, tough guy," Brent said. "We're almost there."

"So, Mimi, what's up with your girl MJ?"

Shaking her head, she elbowed him in the side. "Not a chance in hell."

"What? I'm a nice guy."

Brent coughed and laughed. "That's a good one."

"Come on, Mimi, don't you believe people can change?" Jamal asked.

"People, yes. From the little I know about you, no."

"Don't give him such a hard time," Brent said as he shifted his bags from his left to right hand. "To know Jamal is to somewhat understand him."

"Forget both of y'all," Jamal said. "I don't need help getting your friend."

"Is this sport to you?" Mimi snapped, stopping in her tracks. "I mean, men like you make women just want to pre-record their own personal episode of *Snapped.*"

"That's not right," he said. "I give women what they want and I don't make promises of forever, like some other people." Jamal shot a look at Brent. "Maybe you should write about him."

"Wow. I thought you two were best friends," Mimi said as she took note of the glares between them.

"We're almost home. Why don't we talk about the fact that we might not have enough ice for the beer?" Brent snapped.

Mimi wanted to say something, but seeing Brent's scowl she held her tongue. When they reached the complex, MJ was standing outside talking on her cell phone.

"I can't do this right now," she said as she looked at her friends. MJ shoved her phone in her pocket and forced a smile. "It's about time."

Mimi winked at MJ. "Remember this was your idea."

"Let's get these bags upstairs, because if I know Mimi, there is lobster in there."

"Lobster tails and the Mimi blend of seasonings," Mimi replied.

"All right, let's get cooking," MJ said. Jamal bounded up the steps and grinned at MJ.

"You're a cook, huh?" he asked.

"Sometimes," she replied, smiling brightly at him. Mimi wanted to gag. Part of her wanted to warn her friend, but she also wanted to see MJ get over trifling Nic. So she kept silent. After all, these were adults. And MJ was too smart to fall for Jamal.

"Looks like there's another friendship developing," Brent said as they followed MJ and Jamal inside.

"Whatever," Mimi said.

* * *

Once the groceries were unloaded and the beer and wine were chilling, Mimi and MJ stood at the stove preparing the fish and lobster.

"These guys are actually pretty cool," MJ said as she battered the flounder. "I needed this."

"Are you going to tell me what happened last night or not?" Mimi asked as she blended her seasoning mix.

Sighing, MJ turned to her friend with tears in her eyes. "We slept together and I told him that I was still in love with him."

"No, no, no. Why did you do that?"

"Because it was so amazing and it felt right, but it was wrong. He told me that he wasn't there and probably wasn't going be the man I should give my heart to. While we're lying in bed naked." Tears sprang into her eyes, but MJ didn't let them fall.

"Ouch," Mimi said as she sprinkled the spices on the lobster tails.

"Why is it so hard to find someone to love?" MJ wiped her cheek with the back of her hand and left a streak of cornmeal on her face.

"Because you're looking," Mimi replied. "Just let him find you and it will be incredible."

MJ wiped the mess and the tears from her face as Jamal walked in the kitchen. "Aww hell, what's with the waterworks?" he asked.

"It's the onions, and when are you going to get started on those so-called world-famous hush puppies?" Mimi asked as MJ dropped the first batch of fish in the pan.

"That's why I'm here," he said with a wink. He

crossed over to MJ. "Can we share some space, pretty lady?"

"Sure, but don't get none of that," she said, pointing to his bowl, "on me."

"Messy cooks are the best cooks," he said as he set the bowl on the counter and washed his hands. "And look at you. Still got a little something on your cheek there." Jamal picked up a clean dishtowel and gently wiped her cheek.

Brent stood at the door of the kitchen watching Mimi move around with the skill of a gourmet chef. Seemed as if she had one of the characteristics he wanted in a woman: she could cook. And actually looked like she enjoyed it.

"Mimi, the grill is ready if you are," he said. Brent always wanted his relationships to be about teamwork, and cooking with his boo was always something he'd enjoy. It just never happened. Denisha's idea of a home-cooked meal had been ordering takeout from Boston Market or a soul food restaurant and putting the food on real plates.

"Two seconds, chef," she quipped. "Thanks for hooking that up."

"Anything for you, buddy," Brent said as Mimi crossed over to him with the pan of lobster tails.

Heading for the patio, she glanced out over the city and felt the need to leave again. Sure, she was having fun with Brent, Jamal and MJ, and this was going to be her next blog post. But she felt as if things were getting stale and that wasn't her style.

"What's wrong?" Brent asked when he noticed her far-off look. "You lost something out there or are you thinking about jumping?"

"Funny," she said as she placed the lobster tails on the grill, then sprinkled more of her seasoning mix on them. "I'm just thinking about the future...not with you, but you know, my future someplace else."

"New York, right? That's where all writers want to end up, isn't it?"

"Not me. I'm a Southern belle. I want to walk down the street and have people say hello and have doors held for me. I was thinking about going down to the bayou."

"Louisiana, huh? I went to law school in New Orleans," he said. "As you can see." Mimi thought she heard a bit of pain in his voice, but shrugged it off. Today wasn't the time to have deep conversations about past hurt.

"New Orleans is where I want to be," she said. "But I'm here now and today we eat, drink and play spades."

"Spades, girl, I hope you are ready to lose, big-time."

Mimi folded her arms across her chest. "Are you kidding me? You're about to face the AUC spades champions! MJ and I beat everybody from Morehouse to Morris Brown. They still quiver when they hear our names or the word *Boston*."

"Really cool story, but you haven't come up against me and Jamal. We're the undisputed champions of the world. And we're not taking it easy on y'all because you're girls, either."

"You see a girl out here? Because last time I checked, Mimi Collins is a grown woman who's going to kick your..."

"Are those lobster tails done?" Jamal asked as he and MJ brought out a tray of hot fish and hush puppies.

"Not yet," Mimi said. Pointing her thumb at Brent,

she shook her head. "This one is over here talking about he can beat us in spades."

MJ burst out laughing. "With what army?"

Jamal cleared his throat. "You don't need the army when you have a marine."

"Please, call in the Marines, the Navy and the Air Force, you still don't have a chance against M&M."

Mimi and MJ slapped each other a high five. "They are *not* ready," Mimi said, then turned her attention back to the grill. "They sound just like those dudes from Morehouse who had no idea that we were going to eat their lunch and drink their milk shakes."

"Let's eat so we can teach these ladies a lesson," Brent said as he watched Mimi lift the lobster tails from the grill.

"Get ready to lose, fellas," Mimi said as they sat down to eat.

Chapter 8

The fish and lobster had been a hit, and as much as Mimi didn't want to admit it, Jamal's hush puppies were to die for. But before anyone could dig in for seconds, Brent dropped a deck of cards on the table.

"Time to back up all that talk, ladies," he said.

Jamal rubbed his hands together. "Let's do this."

Mimi laughed. "I've never seen two people so ready to get their asses whipped." MJ gave her friend a high five.

"Let's get it on like Marvin Gaye," she said, then took the deck from the middle of the table. MJ shuffled the cards with the skill of a Vegas dealer.

"Card tricks don't mean you're going to win. Just means you have good hands and watch too much TV," Jamal said as MJ flipped the deck.

"No, our skill means we're going to beat y'all," Mimi said as MJ began dealing the cards.

"No talking across the board, either," Brent shouted.

After four games, Mimi and MJ had backed up their bragging by beating Brent and Jamal. "I want a rematch!" Jamal said as he popped the top on a beer. "Y'all cheated or something."

"Cheated?" Mimi said as she pointed her glass of wine at Brent. "Who held a card back and screamed misdeal?"

"That card fell underneath the table," he joked.

"Fell right out of your hand." She looked over the rim of her wineglass at Brent's smile. He was gorgeous when he smiled. But he was especially sexy when he scowled. While they'd been playing cards, she saw that scowl a lot. And she couldn't help but wonder what kind of faces he'd make late at night while making love. Just the thought of it made her thighs throb.

"It's getting late," Mimi said as she set her glass on the table. "I have to get some writing done this evening."

"Yeah, and I need to see what you're going to say about me," Jamal quipped.

"Anyway," Mimi said as she stood up. "MJ, are you ready?"

"Actually, Jamal and I are going to clean up the kitchen and then hit this new spot he was telling me about when we were frying the fish."

Mimi's mouth formed the shape of an *O*, but she didn't say a word. Maybe Jamal would be MJ's rebound dude for the night, someone who would take her mind off Nic.

That's what she would write about—rebound dates

and how they're not all bad. "You and Brent are welcome to come," Jamal said.

"Nah, I have some briefs to catch up on for Monday. Y'all make sure my kitchen is clean before you leave," Brent said, then rose to his feet. "Mimi, would you like for me to walk you home?"

"Such a gentleman." Mimi rolled her eyes. "I think I'll be safe in the hallway."

"I'm walking you over anyway," he said, then wrapped his arm around her waist. She didn't miss the look that MJ gave her as she and Brent walked out the door.

Alone in the hallway, Mimi had to caution herself not to kiss this man. With his beautiful lips. Full and succulent. This was her friend. Not a friend with benefits, just her friend.

"I had fun today," Brent said as she leaned against her door.

"So did I. We should do it again."

"I know I want some more of those lobster tails. Girl, you have mad skills," he said. "How's your dessert?"

"Play your cards right and you might find out." Mimi winked at him, then unlocked her door. "Good night, Brent."

"Good night, Mimi."

Walking inside, Mimi leaned against the door and sighed. Why was this man getting under her skin? When was the last time she actually cooked for a guy? She normally told men that she couldn't cook.

Mimi headed upstairs to grab her laptop and write her blog post for the evening. She wished that she'd had the guts to invite Brent in for a nightcap, but friends didn't do those things.

Plopping down on the bed, Mimi booted up her computer and got to work on her blog.

Sometimes a rebound isn't a bad thing. There are times when you need to catch another ball to make up for the missed play on the last one. Look, I'm not the biggest sports fan in the world, but let's face it: most people think of dating as a game. No one is really looking to fall in love. If that were the case, there wouldn't be so many single people floating around Atlanta and every other metropolitan city talking about dating games.

So, since dating is a game for most, I say let's play the rebound game. A rebound is great for you as long as you don't get caught up in your feelings. Having fun after a breakup is a good thing. A game of cards with a cute guy doesn't mean you're going to be looking for a diamond at the end of the night. Listening to some music at a trendy hot spot doesn't mean you're in a relationship the next day. Go ahead and rebound. Just remember to keep your feelings in check.

After Mimi found a picture of her favorite Atlanta Hawks player getting a rebound against the Charlotte Hornets, she posted her blog and closed her laptop. It always amazed her that people thought she was constantly on dates or had endless relationships because she talked junk on the internet.

It worked; her blog was popular and people listened to what she said. If only they knew she spent more time alone than with a paramour.

Shrugging off her thoughts, Mimi decided to have

glass of root beer and listen to some jazz. Maybe, she thought, this would take her mind off Brent.

The soft sound of John Coltrane interrupted Brent's reading. Pulling his glasses off, he walked to the door and noticed the music was coming from Mimi's place. He imagined her inside dressed in a silky nightgown, her hair up in a curly bun with a few tendrils around her face. Maybe she was reading or maybe she was swaying to the music as she wrote.

Unable to be satisfied with just his thoughts, Brent crossed the hall and knocked on her door.

A few seconds passed before Mimi opened the door. Brent drank in her image, clad in white cotton shorts and a cropped tank top. "Brent?" she said. "Music too loud?"

Brent closed the space between them and drew Mimi into his arms. Without a word, he kissed her— slow. Deep. Passionate. A moan escaped Mimi's throat before she gave in to the heat of Brent's kiss. His hands roamed her back, reveling in the feel of her soft skin. He wanted to take her upstairs and bury himself deep inside her.

But this wasn't right.

This wasn't how he operated. But damn, Mimi's mouth was magical, her tongue divine. He couldn't stop kissing her if he wanted to.

Mimi pulled back, placing her hand against his chest. "Wh-what was that all about?"

"Something I've wanted to do all day," he said, his voice low and deep. "Hearing Coltrane just pushed me over the edge."

"You know I'm no good for you," Mimi said. "I

don't want the family fantasy you have in your head and I don't do one-night stands."

He nodded. "I just couldn't stop myself. Mimi," he moaned.

"You have to go."

"Listen, I didn't want to come over here and try to make something happen, but you are irresistible."

"Bye, Brent," she said, then turned her mouth up to his and kissed him again. Hard. Deep. Wet. Brent's body felt as if it had been ignited like a stick of dynamite. Then she pressed herself against him, and he was harder than a concrete column. Mimi broke the kiss and they stared into each other's eyes.

"We're playing with fire. How far do you want to take this?" His voice was husky and filled with want.

"If we cross the line, we know that it can't end well," she said. "But you're such a good kisser."

"I'm good at kissing in so many other places, too," he said with a randy wink. "But I'm going to go. I don't think we're ready for anything else right now."

Mimi nodded weakly. Brent turned to the front door, though he wanted nothing more than to taste Mimi again. Looking back at her, he could tell that she was feeling the same way.

"Good night."

Closing the door behind him, Brent knew he'd opened Pandora's box with that kiss. And just like the mythological story, there would be no way to put the lid on that box again.

Chapter 9

Monday morning rolled around too soon for Mimi's taste. But she had a busy day scheduled, thanks to MJ and the blog about Fast Love. She was supposed to join the ladies of *Good Afternoon Atlanta* to talk about the perils of online dating. Waking up at five thirty, she got a short run in before she started doing some research about dating horror stories. Then she tried to think of her own experience on that subject, and other than the Fast Love event, she had none. There was no way, in her opinion, to find love behind a computer screen. She didn't care what the commercials said; online was not the new spot for love.

And neither is your building, she thought as she poured herself a cup of coffee. No matter how hard she tried, Mimi couldn't stop thinking about that kiss. Brent's lips made her see things with him that she hadn't thought about in years. A relationship, waking up every morning in his arms.

"I wonder how he feels about New Orleans," she mused as she fumbled with a package of blueberry muffins.

When she heard a knock at the door, she hoped that it was Brent. Then she looked at her ratty robe and bunny slippers and decided that it might be best if it was just a deliveryman on the other side of the door.

Glancing out the peephole, she saw a tall white guy in a suit standing on the other side of the door holding a small box. She opened the door and smiled at the guy.

"Mimi Collins?"

"Yes," she said.

He handed her the box. "You've been served."

"What?" she snapped as she dropped the box and stepped into the hallway. "What is this about?"

"Guess you should watch what you write about on your blog," he replied snidely.

Mimi rushed him and pushed him against the wall, not noticing that Brent had walked out of his place. "Who in the hell sent you?"

"Lady, get your hands off me. I'm just the process server."

"Who sent you?" she growled.

"Fast Love! Now let me go. I only got fifty dollars for this!"

"Mimi," Brent said as he placed his hand on her arm. "What's going on?"

She turned around and locked eyes with Brent. Immediately, she felt like a wild cavewoman. She dropped her hands from the man's shoulders.

"I ought to sue you, too!"

"Get out of here before I give you a reason!" Mimi snapped. The man took off as if he were The Flash.

"You need to calm down. Where's the document he served you?"

She pointed to the box near her half-open door. "I didn't open it because..."

Brent headed to her door and picked up the box. "Do you mind if I open it?"

"Sure, whatever," she said.

Brent opened the box and pulled out the papers. He read over them and smirked. "I guess Fast Love didn't like your critique of their event and they want to hold you liable."

"It's not my fault they lied. Those bastards!"

"I can help you with this," he said. "If you want me to. Fast Love is seeking damages from you for five million dollars."

Mimi snatched the papers out of his hand. "I don't have that kind of money!"

"I'm sure they know that as well. They want to shut you down. That's usually how these lawsuits work."

"I told the truth and they can't sue me for that. Hello, First Amendment!"

Brent shook his head as he noticed Mimi's scowl.

"Why don't you meet me at my office around two this afternoon and we can get to work on this. Sometimes it just takes a lawyer's voice to get issues like this cleared up."

"Your talk game is that strong?" she quipped.

"I'd like to think so. You know I have an amazing mouth," Brent said, then winked at her. "Nice slippers. See you later. I have to head to court."

Recalling her attire, Mimi felt like a fool. She could

only imagine how she looked to Brent as she accosted the process server. "Oh, my God, I'm an idiot," she whispered as Brent stepped on the elevator.

Brent smiled as he walked into the courtroom. Of course the complainant in the civil case wanted to talk settlement. When Brent uncovered Greta DeVine's history of shoddy work and sexual harassment claims once she was fired, he'd been happy to share that with her attorney.

This hadn't been Greta's first high-profile sexual harassment case, and just like her suit against Atlanta-based computer company DVA, she was going to lose this one as well.

Granted, she was a beautiful woman, but she wasn't as smart as she thought she was. Heading into the conference room with Craig Franklin, CEO of Atlanta Metro Credit Union, Brent knew this was going to be a win for the banker. Craig was one of the few clients he'd represented that he believed hadn't done what he was accused of. Was Craig a ladies' man? Yes, but that was part of Greta's MO. Go after powerful single men with a playboy reputation and sue them for sexual harassment.

"What does she want now?" Craig asked as they stood in the doorway. "My sister told me not to hire that scheming bi…"

"Let me do the talking. You just sit down and scowl. She doesn't have a leg to stand on."

"That's how she got me, those damned legs and short skirts."

"You remind me of my best friend, getting caught thinking with the wrong head," he said as he sat down at the long wooden table and waited for Greta and her attorney. "Didn't y'all get the warning from Bell Biv DeVoe? Never trust a big butt and a smile?"

Craig laughed. "Message received now."

When the duo walked in, Brent stood to shake hands with them, but neither returned his effort.

"Why are we here?" Brent asked as he took his seat.

Susan Chambers, Greta's lawyer, cleared her throat as they sat down. "We're willing to settle."

"Settle," Brent scoffed. "We're not settling, because my client didn't sexually harass Greta. They had an affair that didn't end the way she wanted and Ms. DeVine did what she always does, use the legal system to try to get revenge. We're not doing that and Mr. Franklin isn't paying her for anything."

"You bastard!" Greta snapped. "I'm so sick of you men pretending that you've done nothing wrong when you toy with a woman's emotions."

Susan tugged at Greta's arm. "Let me handle this."

"You're doing a poor job of handling anything! If you want this to disappear, I want one hundred thousand dollars or I will go to the media and let them know who their hero really is."

"Ms. DeVine, that sounds like extortion," Brent said. "Last time I checked, that's a crime."

"F…"

"Greta!" Susan yelled. "Let's just drop the case."

"That is the best idea I've heard all day," Brent said.

"No."

Craig shook his head. "Greta, I'll give you a thousand dollars and a Happy Meal, just leave me alone."

Brent shot his client a cautioning look. "Do we need to leave and let you two non-attorneys hash this out?

Greta," Brent said as he pulled a document from his briefcase and slid it over to her. "If you don't want to find yourself on the other side of a lawsuit, you're going to sign this nondisclosure agreement. You will not speak publicly of Mr. Franklin nor will you disparage him on any form of social media or we will sue you for eighty-five million dollars and go to the police about your extortion attempt." Brent waved his smartphone. "Which was recorded."

Greta rose to her feet and glared at Brent. "You think you're slick, huh?"

"It doesn't matter what I think. Sign the papers and let's stop wasting the court's time."

She signed the papers with a flourish and threw them at Brent before storming out of the conference room. A string of profanities followed Greta down the hall. Susan shook her head as she looked at Brent.

"That was a smooth move," she said. "And if my client wasn't so difficult, I would tell her that your recording wouldn't hold up in court."

Brent smiled. He liked Susan as an attorney; she was tough and usually won her cases, but she wasn't ready to compete with him.

"Susan, I'm surprised you took her case."

"She knows my mother and a few of my aunties," she said with an eye roll. "And she's a great actress. They bought her story and ran a guilt trip on me."

"You're supposed to be stronger than that," he said.

"Teach me about strength over drinks one night. I heard about you and Denisha. I can't say that I'm sorry." Susan winked at him. Brent shook his head as she sauntered out the door. Susan was attractive, smart and accomplished. And before he kissed Mimi, he would've gladly taken her up on her offer for drinks. Maybe even started dating her. But there was something about Mimi that held him back.

"Mimi," he muttered. "Damn it."

"What are you mumbling about?" Craig asked. "We won and a fine legal eagle just handed you the key to her…"

"Thinking with the wrong head will get you every time. Did we not learn a lesson with Greta?" Brent gathered his papers and briefcase. "Next time I see you, I hope it will be about financial planning."

"For sure. As a matter of fact, you need to open an account at the credit union and help me fund some of those scholarships at the Atlanta University Center."

"Let's get together on Monday. Right now, I've got to put another fire out." Brent shook hands with Craig, then headed down the hall. If he could beat the lunch rush, he would make it back to his office in time to review Mimi's blog and the post about Fast Love in depth. He was sure a few of his paralegals probably read Mimi's blog regularly and had heard Rocky his receptionist talk about her online dating experiences. Their input would be vital in getting this case crushed before it even got started. And he'd need that to happen because while Mimi was his client, there could be no more kisses or thoughts of making love to the soulful sax of John Coltrane.

Why did I volunteer to do this? he thought as he walked into the parking garage.

Chapter 10

MJ stood in front of Mimi shaking her head. "I told you that Fast Love blog post was going to get you in trouble. But five million dollars? You're holding like that?"

"Shut up, Mikey," Mimi snapped. "Brent said he can help me and I'm going to let him."

"Help with the case or something else? And the next time you call me *Mikey*, we're fighting."

"Of course the case. Although his lips are magical."

"Wait. What? Y'all kissed?"

Mimi nodded. "After you and Jamal left, I came home, worked on my blog and played some Coltrane. Then he knocked on the door and kissed me."

"Whoa. That was some *Love Jones* melodrama right there. Then, did you…"

Mimi's eyes stretched to the size of quarters. "No!

But I wanted to. Right here on the floor. I was kissed senseless and I didn't even think about Sunday morning."

"That's serious, but you know while he's your attorney you can't do anything with him."

"Well, if he is as good as he says he is, this will all be cleared up with a phone call." Mimi smiled as she thought about feeling the softness of his lips again.

"Earth to Mimi! Wow, this guy must have done a number on you."

"Maybe it's just that I haven't met a man like Brent before. He's different from the typical Atlanta man. Like Jamal, for instance."

"Wait a minute, Jamal's cool," she said. "We had a great time and he was a gentleman. And quite the dancer. And there was no kissing when he dropped me off at my car. He even told me that he wasn't looking for a relationship."

"That's obvious."

"Not really," MJ said. "He likes to have fun, but at least he's honest about it."

"Yeah, but even if a man is honest about wanting to sleep with you whenever he's free, it doesn't mean you don't hurt when the feelings aren't returned."

"Was that a veiled examination of me and Nic? I'm done with that. I've handed his contract off to another one of my employees and I deleted his number from my phone. We're done."

Mimi started to ask for how long, but she realized that she had to meet Brent. "I have to go and get with Brent," she said. "Hopefully traffic isn't going to be that bad."

"You know good and well there is never a time

when traffic isn't bad in midtown. You go and I'll see what I can do as far as your brand goes. The publisher called me. Obviously the news of the suit is making the rounds."

"Damn it," she muttered. "I don't need this, especially since I wanted to pitch a travel book to the publisher."

"What? We didn't talk about that."

"I know. Let's have sushi tonight and I'll go into detail about it."

MJ shot her a questioning look. "Okay," she said. "But that was never in the plan. Your next book was supposed to be based on the blog. That's what we sold the publisher."

"Plans change. See you later," Mimi said, then dashed out the door.

Traffic on Georgia 400 was more like driving around a parking lot. Cars crept along as if they were Hot Wheels being pushed by toddlers. Mimi was about thirty minutes late for her meeting. When she walked into Brent's office, she was extremely impressed. His staff was a mix of young lawyers, men and women. They all had intensity etched on their faces as they moved with the speed of hungry lions around the office. Crossing over to the receptionist's desk, Mimi smiled at her then said, "I have an appointment with Brent Daniels."

The woman looked up at Mimi and smiled. "And your name, ma'am?"

Ma'am? Seriously, do I look that old? she thought. "Mimi Collins."

The woman's eyes stretched incredulously. "*The*

Mimi Collins? Like *The Mis-Adventures of Mimi Collins*?"

"That's me."

"Oh. My. God! I love your stuff. Read your blog every day."

"Thank you." Mimi beamed.

"I'll let Mr. Daniels know you're here," she said as she picked up the phone and handed Mimi a notepad. Placing her hand over the mouthpiece, she whispered, "May I have your autograph?"

Mimi happily scribbled her name on the pad. She listened as the woman told Brent that Mimi was in the lobby. When she told Mimi that Brent would be right out, Mimi handed her the pad. "Thank you for reading," Mimi said.

"Thank you for being so real and fearless!"

Mimi pulled out her cell phone. "Want to take an us-ie?"

She tilted her head to the left. "He wouldn't like that."

Mimi looked up and locked eyes with Brent. And damn did he look good. Dressed in a charcoal suit and a peach tie, he looked even sexier than he had in the hallway at home. Was he wearing that suit before? Mimi couldn't remember because she'd been so angry and appalled by her actions that she hadn't noticed.

Now she saw it all. And he was a sight to behold. "Hi," Mimi said.

"You're late," he said, then smirked.

"Traffic," she said after learning to breathe again. "But I'm here now. Let's get this madness over with."

Brent nodded. "We need to talk about this. Follow me to my office." Mimi watched him as he strode across the floor. He walked with confidence and purpose. Everyone seemed to be in such awe of him. Mimi was no exception. Brent at home was totally different from Brent in the office. Gone was the killer smile that Mimi saw as they played cards. He was a man about his business.

Once they reached his office, Brent held the door for Mimi and turned to his petite blonde secretary.

"Anita, hold my calls," he said briskly.

"Yes, sir."

Mimi walked in behind Brent and was impressed again. From his massive mahogany desk to the wall of legal books behind it and the windows looking out over the city, she felt as it she was in the presence of power. This Fast Love thing would be over before it started. He offered Mimi a seat.

"Mimi, I reread your Fast Love blog. Can you prove everything you said?" he asked.

"Yes, but what does that have to do with anything?"

"It's harsh, Mimi. Their case has some merit."

She leaned back in the chair. "What happened to 'all they need to hear is a lawyer's voice and it will be done'? That event was bogus. That company is preying on single women trying to find love."

"That may be true, but how is this any different from any other online dating site?"

"You're defending them?"

"They want to meet. Mimi, do you realize how popular your blog is? I talked to a few of the ladies here who live and die by your recommendations. They're just a sample. As Spider-Man said, with great power comes responsibility."

"Really?" she asked.

"Maybe that was a little much, but you're a taste-maker and your words carry power. Did you meet Rocky out front?"

"Rocky? Oh, the receptionist. Yes."

"She gave me a crash course on Mimi Collins this morning," Brent said as he leaned forward in his chair. "You speak your mind as if you're talking to your girl-friends. That's what she said. The only problem with that is it's as if you have about fifteen million girl-friends and that has allegedly hurt Fast Love's bot-tom line." Brent turned the computer screen around and showed Mimi the email he'd received from Fast Love's attorney. Mimi glanced at the metrics show-ing how the enrollment on the site had dropped since Mimi's blog went viral.

"So? They lied. They set up women to meet these men who were expecting sex, and what if someone had been raped?"

"Good point. But can you prove it?"

Mimi stroked her forehead, then she remembered the email. "Hell yes!" Digging her smartphone out of her purse, she searched for the random guy's email that she'd forwarded to herself.

Mimi held her phone underneath his nose. "This is what the men got and it was totally different from the email the women received."

"This changes everything," Brent said as he read the email. "Do you have your original email?"

"Of course I do," Mimi said. "So can we put this thing to bed now? I have to go record a talk show about online dating in an hour."

"No," he said.

Mimi rose to her feet. "You can't tell me what to do."

"You're right, but I'm advising you not to say anything about online dating until this is wrapped up. Their lawyers are going to be watching you and your blog. Anything you type, text or tweet will be held against you. I think you should take a hiatus."

"Are you going to pay my rent? This blog is my life. These media appearances mean more page views, more revenue, more advertisers…"

"More lawsuits," Brent exclaimed. "Mimi, why do you hide behind the internet?"

"What? I'm not hiding at all."

"Really, Mariah?"

Mimi stopped in her tracks. "Excuse me?"

"I'm not telling you anything I wouldn't tell another client," he said as he touched her shoulders. Mimi shrugged out of his embrace.

"You volunteered for this."

"And I wouldn't be doing my job if I didn't try to stop you from self-destructing. Why do you go so hard on the internet and think that no one will retaliate? Do you realize your influence on people?"

"If I'm telling the truth, isn't the law on my side?" Mimi asked.

"This is a civil case. The rules are different, but you have the main thing you need to win."

"And that is?"

Brent gave her a half smile. "Me. As long as you follow my advice."

Mimi moved closer to the door. "I'll take that under advisement." Her glance fell on his lips. "Maybe we should seal it with a kiss?"

He took a step back. "As much as I'd love to, things

have changed. While I'm representing you, we can't cross that line."

Mimi placed her hand on the doorknob. "That's why lines are there, to be crossed."

"Ever think that's why you're being sued for five million dollars? Mimi, sometimes you have to follow the rules and don't get to make them up as you go along."

Gritting her teeth, Mimi held her tongue. "Goodbye, Attorney Daniels." She stormed out of the office, confused by her attitude. Why was she upset with the man for doing his job? A job he volunteered for. She'd just fire him and find another lawyer to get this stupid suit tossed out. She had a good mind to walk back into his office and end the business relationship right now. But the look from his secretary stopped her from being dramatic.

"Miss Collins," the woman said.

"Yes?" Mimi forced a smile at her.

"I just wanted to tell you how much I enjoy your writing. You're so honest and raw."

"Thank you," she said, then shook the woman's hand. "I try not to disappoint."

"I can't wait for your next book," she said.

Mimi smiled and then locked eyes with Brent as he walked out of his office. "Thank you, Anita," she said. "I'll make sure you get an autographed copy."

The woman beamed. "Thank you so much!"

"Mimi," Brent said. His deep voice sending chills down her spine. "Can we talk?"

"I have to go, Mr. Daniels. But please let me know when the meeting with Fast Love will be. I want to make sure I'm ready." Turning on her heels, Mimi sauntered out the door.

* * *

Brent watched the sway of Mimi's hips and thought of palm trees in a gentle breeze. That didn't keep him from thinking about making love to Mimi underneath palm trees. This woman was all wrong for him.

Brash. Opinionated. And she didn't listen. He had no doubt that she was going to do that interview.

"Mr. Daniels," Anita said, breaking into his thoughts. "Rocky says your next appointment is here."

"Give me five minutes," he said then retreated to his office.

Mimi did what Brent thought she was going to do and headed to the *Good Afternoon Atlanta* studio. She was going to tell the hosts about the lawsuit and tell them that her attorney advised her not to talk about specific online sites. That should keep Brent's boxers from getting in a bunch. If it didn't, so what. As she walked through the doors, her phone rang.

She was happy and disappointed to see that it was MJ and not Brent. "Hello?"

"What are you doing?" MJ asked. "Because I just called *Good Afternoon Atlanta* and they said you're still doing the show."

"Yes, I am," Mimi said.

"Are you crazy?"

"No, but I can't go silent on my blog and in the media. I don't care what you and Brent say."

"What did Brent say?" MJ asked.

"That I should take a hiatus."

"I was going to suggest the same thing. Re-blog some of your older popular posts and wait this thing out. Mimi, you can't afford to have this get out of hand before the second book comes out. And the movie deal has not been finalized. Suppose the studio decides not to go forward with you because of this?"

She sighed and started to tell MJ that she wasn't going on the show and saying anything about Fast Love, but that would've been a lie.

"I'm not going to let them attack my character when Fast Love is wrong for their marketing. What if a woman at that event had been raped?"

"But no one was."

"That we know of. Who's to say they won't do this again?"

"You think you're going to stop them? Mimi…"

"What if I can? I'm tired of people and companies taking advantage of women looking for love. I speak out and get sued. There's something that needs to be said about that."

"Okay, if that's what you think," MJ said. "But you're making it much harder on yourself to do the book you want to do and keep from having to pay money you don't have. I've known you long enough to know that you're going to do what you want, good advice be damned."

"Thank you for respecting that," she said. "I'll call you later." Mimi ended the call, then walked in the studio. When one of the producers grabbed her and told her that Fast Love's lawyer was going to be on the show and asked her if she had an attorney of her own, Mimi knew she might be in over her head.

"Let me make a phone call," she said as she pulled out her cell phone and called Brent.

Chapter 11

It was the third time that Brent had ignored Mimi's call as he spoke to Myra Ellington. Their consultation should've been over an hour ago, but the elder Myra Ellington thought she was in 1950 and still a sex symbol.

"Brent," the senior citizen purred. "We can make magic together and you can get my company back for me."

"That is the plan, ma'am," he said.

"My mother is ma'am. I'm Myra," she said with what she probably thought was a sexy smile.

"Well, Miss Myra, I'm here to help you get your company back," he said as he shook her hand. His phone rang again and he wanted to answer Mimi, but Myra wouldn't let his hand go.

"I'm putting my trust in you, Brent," she said as she released his hand. "But I need to know that I'm a priority." Myra shot a glance at his phone.

"All of my clients are a priority," he said.

"But I'm giving you a million-dollar retainer. Don't fail me," she warned, then rose to her feet.

"If I were in the business of failing, you wouldn't be here," he said, then picked up his cell phone as Myra headed for the door.

Not two seconds after Myra walked out the door, Mimi called again. This time, he picked up the phone.

"Mimi, what's going on?"

"Can you come to the *Good Afternoon Atlanta* studio? Fast Love's attorney is here. They kind of set me up."

Brent sighed. "I thought I told you to cancel the interview."

"And I said I'd take it under advisement. Can you get here and help me?"

Brent glanced at his watch. "How long to I have?"

"About twenty minutes," she said. He could almost hear her smile.

"Mimi, why don't you tell them that you aren't going to go on the show because you can't discuss pending litigation?"

"Because I'm not a punk and I didn't do anything wrong. You said you'd help me," she said. "Are you going to keep your word?"

"Is this live or recorded?"

"Recorded, I think. Brent, I need you."

Sighing, he replied, "I'm on my way." Maybe it had been the way Mimi said she needed him that prodded him into action or maybe he was just being a damned fool. Any other client who'd ignored his advice, he'd drop like a bad habit. He couldn't do that to Mimi.

Still, after this interview, he was going to lay down

the rules and if she didn't follow them, he would drop the case.

"And that might be the best thing I can do for my sanity," he muttered as he grabbed his jacket and keys.

Mimi stalked back and forth like a caged lioness as she waited for Brent to show up. She was mad and felt as if she'd been ambushed because the show wasn't supposed to be about this stupid lawsuit. Locking eyes with the petite blonde lawyer, Mimi wanted nothing more than to throw a drink at her. But this wasn't a tawdry reality show and she had more class than that.

"Where is Brent?" she mumbled as she looked down at her watch. A producer crossed over to Mimi.

"Miss Collins, we're going to have to get started with the taping soon," she said as she pressed the earpiece in her ear. "Yes. I'm with her right now. I don't see anyone with her. I'm standing outside the studio. Okay, I'll ask." She looked at Mimi as she remembered that Mimi had been standing there.

"Umm, is your attorney coming?"

"I'm right here," Brent's sexy voice said from behind them. Mimi felt tingles in her thighs when she heard him speak. The producer didn't even try to keep her composure.

"Oh my freaking goodness! It's Brent Daniels. Brent Daniels is her lawyer."

Brent glanced at Mimi. "Who is she talking to?" he asked.

"The people in the control room or the voices in her head. I don't know, but I'm so happy to see you."

"I started not to come. This is a bad idea, Mimi."

"They tried to set me up. I didn't know these clowns were going to be here."

Brent placed his arm around Mimi's waist and moved her out of the way of a speeding cameraman. "You shouldn't be here, but since we're here and it's going to be recorded, let me do the talking. That's not up for negotiation."

She gave him a mock salute. "Yes, sir."

He smirked at her. "You're something else, you know that."

"And you like it."

Brent was about to say something when the producer tugged at his arm. "We're ready," she said. "And Mr. Daniels, you look even better in person. Maybe once this is over, we can do a one-on-one interview about your career." She handed him a card and flashed her pearly whites. Mimi wanted to snatch that card from Brent's hand and toss it in the trash. Wait, why was she acting like a jealous girlfriend or something? If Brent wanted to have a sit-down with this chick, then that was up to him.

"I'm not one to talk about myself," he said as he pocketed the card. "But I'll keep your offer in mind."

"Well, we could at least meet for drinks," she said, then winked at him as they walked over to the host table.

"Mimi," Carrington Clarke, one of the hosts, said. "Glad to see you."

"You couldn't have warned me?" Mimi asked the woman whom she'd considered a friend.

"Wasn't my idea." She nodded toward Kimberlin Thompson, the other host. "She saw the news about the lawsuit online and called Fast Love. They were happy to come on and confront you."

"A text, a call, anything would've had me prepared."

"Or you could've canceled your appearance like I advised you to do," Brent said.

Carrington glanced at Brent. "Well, Mimi, I see you pulled out the big guns. Mr. Brent Daniels, attorney-at-law."

"I'm glad I don't believe my own press," Brent said.

"They call you Mr. Cannot Lose. I know you listen even if you don't believe it." She looked at Mimi. "How did you two meet?"

"Not on Fast Love," Mimi quipped. Brent brought his lips to her ear and she nearly shivered.

"This is why you're going to let me talk and you're just going to sit there and look pretty."

She turned to face him and their lips nearly touched. Mimi took a step back. "That wasn't sexist at all."

"Let me work, okay," he said.

She nodded and they took their seats.

Brent crossed his legs and listened to the Fast Love attorney, Judith Bright, talk about how Mimi's storytelling about the event hurt the company.

"Maybe Miss Collins is just upset because she didn't meet anyone at the event."

"Are you serious?" Mimi exclaimed. Brent placed his hand on her knee.

"Judith, that was a baseless claim, and if my client takes a page out of your book, then I'm seeing a lawsuit against you. Fact, Mimi told the truth about your event. You should be talking to the marketing company, which sent out two different emails to the women and men who signed up for your event," Brent said. "So, are you going to apologize to my client or do I need to serve you?"

Mimi nodded her head and almost wanted to fist-bump Brent, but the cautioning look he shot her made her ease back into her chair.

"Well," Judith stammered.

"And on that note, we're going to a commercial break," Kimberlin said. Then she turned to Brent. "You're so hard-core."

"I'm going to get some water," he said as he rose to his feet. He was getting bored with the interview, but it wasn't lost on him that Fast Love didn't have a case. They had conjecture. Mimi wasn't going to pay them a dime. Glancing at her as she crossed her legs, he couldn't wait for this case to be over. He wanted those legs wrapped around him while he drove deep inside her. Walking away, he went to the craft table and grabbed a bottle of water. Removing the cap, he downed the ice-cold contents and hoped it would cool the desire building inside him. The water wasn't enough. He wanted the forbidden fruit that sat at the table. He wanted Mimi. The producer walked over to him and tapped his elbow.

"We're ready to start taping," she said. "Even if you don't want to do the interview, we should have dinner."

"Maybe not," he said as he returned to the table.

"Are we ready?" Carrington asked.

"How much longer are we going with this back-and-forth? Fast Love and its representatives are clearly trying to use Mimi Collins's blog to acquire more victims."

Mimi placed her hand to her mouth. She was impressed in a big way. Brent didn't mince words at all. "From what I've seen," Brent continued, "Fast Love was in a lot of trouble before Mimi Collins exposed their bogus scam."

"I'm out of here," Judith said. "I'm not going to sit here and let this man accuse us of…"

"Lying?" Mimi said. She closed her eyes when Brent placed his hand on her shoulder.

"Well, there you have it, Atlanta," Carrington said. "And we will see you tomorrow."

"And we're clear," the producer said.

"Where do you get off accusing our company of being liars?" Judith railed at Mimi. "That's slander."

"That will be edited," Brent said, then gave Carrington a pointed look.

She shrugged.

Mimi began. "Why hide the truth?" Brent touched her elbow.

"Stop. We'll do our talking in court."

"I, uh, have been authorized to take a settlement," Judith stammered. "One hundred thousand dollars and a retraction."

"You must have been bounced on your head as a baby," Mimi exclaimed.

Brent shot her a look that screamed *be quiet*. "I don't understand why you think Ms. Collins should retract her blog post. Did she say anything that wasn't true?"

"Well, umm, listen. That is our offer, take it or we'll see you in court."

Brent folded his arms across his chest, then laughed. "You and I both know Fast Love doesn't want this to go to court. There are emails. There is proof that everything Mimi wrote was true. And she runs a blog. Not the *New York Times*. Her opinion is the reason she was invited to your event. Now, since you don't like what she said and what her thoughts were, you want to act like a spoiled brat. The law is not on your side. And if you want to press this issue, there is a countersuit that we can go for. And Mimi isn't going to settle."

Mimi smiled at Judith. "I'm out of here," she said. Turning toward the exit, Mimi was impressed and pissed. Brent handled the interview and the other attorney like a pro, but his quip about her blog not being the *New York Times* made her feel insignificant.

It may not be rocket science but it was hers, and Mimi took her work seriously. By the time Brent caught up with her, she was seething.

"Mimi, hold up," he said, reaching out and touching her shoulder. She turned around and glared at him.

"What? I'm in a hurry to go and do my unimportant work. It's not as if I'm writing an exposé for the *New York Times*," she said as she gripped her car door handle.

"Really?"

"Yes, really," she spat. "I'm sorry that I don't fit into that little mold you want to pour women into. I'm me and I won't be anyone else. And let's keep in mind that you volunteered. I didn't ask for your help."

"I didn't mean to offend you, but I was trying to make a point."

"That I don't matter? Was that your point?"

"Mimi, you're blowing this way out of…"

She snatched her door open, nearly hitting him. "I have to go," she snapped, then tucked herself inside her car.

Speeding out of the parking lot, Mimi knew she

had no right to be so angry with Brent. He was trying to make a point to the Fast Love lawyer and provide doubt that a civil jury might consider.

Didn't matter. She had so many naysayers in her ear that when she started making a profit from her blog, it was a relief.

Then her popularity grew and the doubters disappeared. Mimi felt as if she had a voice that mattered and to hear Brent say those things brought up old insecurities that she'd thought had been long buried. Speaking of buried, Mimi knew she needed to quash her thoughts of naked Brent making love to her.

If she was honest with herself, she would admit that she was confusing business and personal. Right now, though, Mimi wanted to wallow in her feelings and write, while chomping on something chocolate. She headed for Amélie's in midtown to get her favorite treat and grab a corner table to write. Mimi turned her cell phone off because she didn't want to be bothered with anyone—especially Brent.

Chapter 12

Brent stormed into his office. He'd called Mimi three times and his calls went straight to voice mail. Was she really that petty? They still had business together even if her feelings were hurt.

Granted, he was a bit harsh, but he was trying to make a point to Fast Love's lawyer. She had to admit that she wasn't a journalistic source of information. But diminishing her was the last thing he wanted to do. He had no idea why she took what he said so personally.

Just as he was about to call Mimi again, his phone rang. Glancing at the caller ID, he saw that it was an unknown number. Brent started to ignore the call, but since he had clients who called from different locations, he answered.

"This is Brent."

"Brent Daniels Jr.?" a female voice asked.

"Yes. Who's this?"

"My name is Dr. Karen Alexander. I'm calling about your father."

"I don't have a father," Brent snapped.

"Mr. Daniels, your father is dying, and since you're a family member listed on his emergency contacts, it's my duty to tell you about your father's health."

"I don't care about…"

"Mr. Daniels, I know you may have some issues with your father for whatever reason, but the man is dying. Your namesake, and if you don't at least see him, you're going to regret it."

Brent ended the call and tossed his phone across his office. Seeing his father was not an option and if he died, so be it. Walking over to his desk, he buzzed Anita.

"Yes, sir?" she asked.

"I'm taking the rest of the afternoon off. I will have my cell if it is an emergency," Brent said. "I'm heading out the back."

"Is everything all right?"

"I just need some time. If Mimi Collins calls, please find me."

"Yes, sir," Anita said.

Brent picked up his cell phone, then headed down in his private elevator. When he saw Jamal calling him, he decided to ignore the call. Part of him wondered if he'd been the one who gave the prison doctor his information. "Why does this even matter to him?" he muttered as the doors of the elevator opened in the parking deck. Brent needed a drink. But since the last thing he needed was a DUI, he drove home and decided to head to one of the bars within walking distance.

* * *

Mimi was about to post her blog about her kiss with Brent when her cell phone rang. Thinking it was Brent again, she started to ignore it, but she looked down and saw it was MJ.

"What's up?" she said when she answered.

"I heard about the taping at *Good Afternoon Atlanta*. You're lucky to have Brent on your side," MJ said.

"Forget Brent!"

"Wait. What? Carrington said he was awesome on and off camera."

"Whatever. Anyway, what do you want? I'm writing."

"Umm, I'm guessing something happened that Carrington didn't see. Where are you?"

"At Amélie's."

"I'm not too far from you. I'll meet you there and don't publish anything," MJ said. "You and your fast fingers are how we got in this mess."

"This is not a 'we' thing. This is about me. And I'm pretty damned sick of people telling me how I should run my blog!"

"Mimi, calm down, and I'm not telling you how to run anything."

"I'm sorry. I'll be here," she said. After hanging up with MJ, Mimi read over her blog post.

Why is it so hard for two people to admit that they like each other? This is what we want when we date, right? We want to meet that one person who gives you butterflies and makes your knees quake with one kiss.

Look, I've met that guy. He's amazing, smart and everything that a woman could want. Everything I said I didn't want. Marriage, commitment and a future—

with one man. Now, I enjoy dating. And dating does not mean you're sleeping with everyone who takes you to Starbucks! But this guy, this strong, professional man, is just what we all yearn for. I mostly yearn for his touch and the taste of his lips. But he is so damned structured. He's that guy who has to follow all of the rules and regulations—that's just not me. I color outside the lines, and as much as I want him, I can't conform. I can't do what he wants me to do.

Relationships have never been my thing. My mistakes are why I can write this blog. I do trial and error. I don't want to have this happen with Mr. Law and Order. Did I mention that all of that sexiness is my neighbor? Even if I wanted to avoid him, I couldn't. The thing is, I don't want to. I want to feel his arms wrapped around me, want to feel his lips pressed against mine, and maybe I want to spend more than just one night with him.

Maybe.

Okay, I do. But why should I pour myself into something that is doomed from the start?

Mimi tapped her nails on the edge of her computer, toying with whether to post the blog or not. She saved the draft and took a sip of her soda. This was way too personal.

But it was real. Too real. Mimi returned to her blog and wrote about feeling restless and wanting to go to New Orleans. It was uninspired, but she tried to make it funny. After reading over that draft, she figured talking about wanting to travel would make her pitch to the publisher about a travel book a little better. After searching for some links to some off-the-beaten-path spots in New Orleans, Mimi finally had a blog she could publish and not get sued for.

"What are you doing?" MJ asked when she walked up behind her friend.

"Working."

"What was that blog about?"

"New Orleans."

"Whew," MJ said as she crossed over to the empty chair across from Mimi.

"Didn't I tell you that I'm getting sick of people telling me how to run my fu—"

"Calm down, Me. I talked to the publisher today and we have a problem."

Mimi sighed. "Really? As if this day can't get any worse."

"The deal is on hold until your case with Fast Love is resolved. They don't want to have the liability if…"

"You know what, forget it. I can publish my book my damn self," Mimi railed. She slammed her laptop shut. "I'm going home."

"No, you're going to calm down and we're going to have sushi. How does that sound?"

Mimi rolled her eyes. "Whatever."

"Okay, so what is the real deal?"

Mimi tucked her laptop in her case, then faced MJ. "Brent."

"I figured as much. What did he do? Kiss you again? Feel you up at the taping?"

Mimi folded her arms across her chest and glared at her friend. "Just like you, he has ideas on what I should do with my blog. And you know what he said to Fast Love's stupid attorney?"

"Well, I wasn't there, so are you going to share?" MJ asked, not trying to hide her amusement at all.

"He said my blog is not a real journalistic source and they shouldn't take me seriously."

MJ burst out laughing. And Mimi tossed a napkin at her. "You think that's funny?" she snapped at her friend.

"Actually, I do. I've never seen you so upset about someone's opinion like this. I mean, you have had many doubters in your past and proved them wrong. Why does Brent Daniels's opinion carry so much weight?"

Mimi closed her eyes. "Because I really like him. And maybe I'm hoping that if he stops being my lawyer we can move past this awkward stage in our whatever this is."

"Whoa," MJ said, leaning back in her chair. "That is the last thing I really expected to hear."

Opening her eyes, Mimi shook her head. "He's just really not my type. He's Mr. Buttoned Up, I can't explain it."

"You're horny, he kissed you and shook up your hormones. Mimi, he is one of the best lawyers in the country. You need to keep your thighs together and let him fix this mess. Then proceed to do whatever you two want to do."

"Okay, that's not what I expected to hear from you."

"Jamal and I have been talking about this dating scene and why everyone is so confused. No one is honest about what he or she wants."

"I've been saying that for years, but as soon as a man says it, you believe it?"

"No, after getting my feelings stomped on for the last time, I'm finally ready to receive it. I thought helping Nic would make him fall in love with me and see what I have to offer."

Mimi shrugged because she knew MJ didn't feel as if she was revealing some big news. "Well…"

"Oh, hush," MJ said. "Point is, if you want that man, then have him. But what does this mean for you being restless in Atlanta, though?"

"That hasn't changed. When this nightmare is over, I'm still out of here."

"So, why would you start something that you can't finish? I doubt Brent is going to leave his career to follow you around the world."

"I don't expect him to," she said. "I don't want to be Mrs. Brent Daniels. I think I just want to jump his bones and move on."

"Come on," MJ said as she rose to her feet. "Let's go get California rolls."

Brent walked into Gekko Sushi ready to huddle up with some sake and silence. He'd decided not to be a neighborhood barfly and drove to the restaurant instead of walking to a bar. Brent had made it clear to Jamal that he didn't want to talk to him for the rest of the day and his mother made it crystal clear that she didn't care if Brent Sr. dropped dead or not.

"Son," she'd said, "your father was a selfish bastard and did a horrible thing. He hurt a lot of people. I know you need closure with him and you want my permission to care. You make your peace with him. I did that years ago."

"What do you mean?"

"I visited him in prison once. I needed to know why he destroyed our family."

Brent had taken a deep breath. He had no idea that his mother had seen his father after he'd been convicted.

"What did he say?"

"Nothing. He sat there and looked at me as if I was a stranger. It was as if I were talking to a brick wall. When I stood to leave, he told me never come back. That if I'd been the woman he thought I was, we could've made a difference in the city of Atlanta. But I was just a damned schoolteacher who didn't know how to take power. When he said that, I realized that he never loved me. He married me because of my family's ties in the Atlanta social scene. The only thing that man ever gave me that was worth anything is you. That's why I spent all of those years in a loveless marriage."

"Ma," Brent had intoned.

"So, you can see him before it's too late and get what you need."

"Maybe I don't need anything," he said.

"Son," she'd said with a sigh. "You've been angry and holding on to it for years. You've lived your life to prove you are nothing like your father. You need to step all the way out of his shadow."

"Thanks, Ma," he said.

"And son, I'm proud of you. You are the man I raised and you're a good man," she said. "You'd be even better if you came to visit a little more often."

Brent laughed. "All right, Ma. I'll see if I can come this weekend."

"Well, this weekend isn't good for me. I'm going fishing with Nathan Collier."

"Who is Nathan Collier?"

"Bye, son," she said, then disconnected the call.

Thinking about his mother dating and moving on with her life made him think of Mimi. What was it about this woman that drove him so crazy? The kiss. The taste of her lips was emblazoned on his soul. He should've considered that before volunteering to help her with the Fast Love case.

Reaching for his phone, he dialed Mimi's number again. Voice mail. Hanging up, he called Judith Bright, Fast Love's lawyer. It was time to put this case to bed.

"This is Judith."

"Judith, Brent Daniels. I want to talk to you about your case against Mimi Collins," he said.

"We made an offer and you rejected it. I don't know what we have to talk about."

Telephone tough girl, huh, he thought as he listened to her talk. She sounded a lot more confident than she had in the studio.

"Your offer was laughable. Why don't you drop this?"

"She slandered my client on her blog. Millions of people read it and Fast Love's bottom line is suffering."

"Fast Love is suffering because of poor marketing. I tell you what, we can do this the easy way or the hard way."

"The hard way?" she asked.

"Mimi has strong media connections and if this is tried in the court of public opinion, then your client is really going to lose money."

"Not if we get an injunction against her!"

"Are you forgetting that we have evidence that shows Fast Love put women's lives in danger? Mimi has both emails that were sent out."

"Give me a day to call you back."

"That's all you have, or I'm going to unleash Mimi and allow her to go on the media tour of death for Fast Love. Think about it, she's already cost you a good deal of money. How much more do you want to lose?"

"Is that a threat?"

"Not at all. That is a promise. I look forward to hearing from you tomorrow," he said, then ended the call. As Brent turned around, he saw Mimi and MJ walk into the restaurant. When their eyes locked, he smiled at Mimi. The scowl on her face gave him a brief pause, but he crossed over to her anyway.

Of all the sushi joints in Atlanta, Mimi had to walk into the one where the man who'd caused her emotional breakdown was and he had the gall to be coming her way.

I don't want to be an adult, I don't want to not slap him in the face. Why is he so sexy with that tie askew? she thought as he planted himself in front of her.

"Nice to see you, Mimi," he said. "Especially since you won't answer my calls."

"Been busy writing some unimportant drivel on that blog of mine," she said.

"Your sarcasm is enticing," he quipped with a smile. Mimi wanted to kiss and punch him at the same time. "I have some good news for you about the Fast Love case. Tomorrow we should hear if they are going to drop their claim."

Now she wasn't mad, she was impressed and didn't stop herself from hugging him. "Brent, you're amazing."

Pulling back from her, he smiled. "I try to be. Mimi, I didn't want to…"

"Excuse me," the hostess said. "Do you all need a table?"

"Yes," Brent said. "We're celebrating tonight."

Mimi furrowed her brow. "We're not that cool yet," she said.

"We will be once I tell you how we're going to proceed with this if they don't give us what we want."

"If Mimi doesn't want to talk about this, I do," MJ said, then turned to the hostess. "Table for three."

"Follow me," she said as she grabbed three menus and led them to a secluded table in the rear of the restaurant. "I think this will be best for you."

"Thank you," MJ said as she watched the heated look Mimi speared Brent with. "We're going to need a lot of sake."

The woman nodded. "I'll send your waitress over with it, and good luck."

"Thanks," MJ said, then sat down across from Mimi, forcing her and Brent to sit side by side.

"Really?" Mimi said with a shake of her head.

"Shush, let the man speak. Brent, how have you ended this madness?"

"I told Judith, the lawyer for Fast Love, that I was going to let Mimi be Mimi and try this thing in the court of public opinion. I could hear her heels quaking. Your voice, Mimi, scares people."

"Yes, my unimportant not-the-*New-York-Times* voice," Mimi said.

"Let it go, Me," MJ said. "And we were going to protect Mimi's brand anyway, so how does this change anything?"

"They have twenty-four hours to shut down the suit

or Mimi goes viral. And I know you two can make that happen in about fifteen minutes."

Mimi's frost toward Brent was starting to melt. Maybe he did get it and… Why did he have to be so sexy when he smiled? *Stop looking at him like some lovesick teenager,* she chided as she turned her attention to the menu.

"Yes, we can, right, Mimi?" MJ asked.

She snapped her head up. "Sure. But weren't you just telling me that I should scale back on my blog?" Mimi asked, looking pointedly at Brent.

"And I was wrong, for the second time today," he said, then placed his hand on her shoulder. Mimi shivered with delight at his touch and hated it because she knew all she could do was fantasize about that kiss and where he could put those hands.

"I'm glad you can admit that you were wrong," she said. "But what if they don't settle?"

"They will. The bad press would kill them and…" Brent's phone chimed. He looked down at the screen and muttered a curse. "I have to take this."

When he walked away from the table, MJ broke out into laughter. "You two are ridiculous."

"What do you mean?"

"So obvious that you want each other."

"And while I'm his client that can't happen."

"Which is why he is probably working overtime to get this Fast Love case settled. That man is smitten with your evil ass. Why are you giving him such a hard time? And don't tell me it's about what he said earlier."

Mimi sighed as she saw the waitress approaching the table with sake. She knew she was going to need a drink. "I like him."

"Okay," MJ said as the waitress set the bottle of sake on the table. Turning to the smiling woman, MJ said, "We're going to need a few minutes."

"Let me know when you're ready," she replied, and walked away.

Mimi glanced at Brent, who had walked to the front of the restaurant to take his call. "But he is not what I need," she said, then poured a glass of sake.

"How do you know that?" MJ took the glass away. "You need to be sober for this."

Mimi rolled her eyes. "Because he's Mr. Happily-Ever-After. Two point three kids and a big house out in the burbs."

"Why do you act like I'm one of your blog readers? I know you, Mariah. I know you want the same kind of love your parents have, but you've told yourself that you can't have that because of one heartbreak."

"You're out of line."

"No, you're out of your mind. He's not your ex. Stop being a punk, Mimi."

"I'm far from one. But I'm not going to pretend I want to be some Atlanta housewife when I want to travel and write."

"So you can't have love because of that? You're crazy. You just don't want to risk falling in love because you think you're this spunky image you portray online. This is real life, Mimi. Live."

Mimi reached for her sake, but MJ drank it. "And this is coming from the woman who spent years in love with a man who…"

"Stop. You can easily point out other people's faults, but never see your own. Yes, I fell in love with Nic and it didn't work out. But I'm not stupid enough to think that's how things are going to go with the next man I meet. Did I waste too much time with him, yes. But I'm off that horse and moving forward. When are you going to do the same?"

Mimi closed her eyes and let MJ's words sink in. Was she moving forward or running away?

"Is he dead?" Brent asked the doctor.

"No, Mr. Daniels, your father isn't dead. But I wanted to give you a call to see if you had changed your mind about visiting him."

"I do need to see him, but I have a case that I'm finalizing right now."

"The sooner you come, the better. His health is deteriorating and I don't want you to miss your last moments with him," she said.

"Why do you care so much?"

"Excuse me?"

"Why does it matter to you if I see a dying inmate?"

"It—it doesn't. But this is more about family than it is anything else. Can you live with yourself if you let your father die alone?"

"Yes, I can. I will come visit but the constant calls aren't going to change anything." Brent glanced over his shoulder. "Why is this so important to you?"

"Because I'm watching your father suffer and he wants to see his sons."

"Sons? What are you talking about?"

"That's why it's important for you to see your father before it is too late."

"I'll see if I can get there in the morning," Brent said, then ended the call. Taking a deep breath, he headed back to the table with Mimi and MJ, ready to pretend that he wasn't pondering what the doctor said. Sons?

Chapter 13

MJ kicked Mimi underneath the table. "You're acting like a child."

"Stop it. I'm getting really tired of you taking his side."

"Mimi, can't you see that this man is turning himself inside out to settle this case for you? You aren't crazy enough to not understand why."

"MJ, I don't want to get hurt and I..." When she noticed Brent returning to the table, Mimi stopped talking. Looking at him, Mimi saw something in his eyes. It looked like hurt.

"Brent, are you all right?" she asked as he sat down.

"Yeah."

She placed her hand on top of his. "Are you sure?"

He smiled, but it didn't reach his eyes. "Mimi, I might not be the best company tonight."

"What's going on? I know I…"

He shook his head and leaned into her. "I just got a call that has me a bit out of sorts and I don't want to put a damper on your dinner."

"Want to talk about it?"

He shook his head and was about to tell her that he was going to leave when MJ's cell phone rang.

"Hey, Jamal," she said when she answered. "Yeah. I'm with both of them. We're at Gekko."

Brent waved his hand trying to stop her from telling Jamal anything. MJ rolled her eyes.

"By all means, come join us."

Brent groaned as MJ ended the call.

"What's wrong with you?" she asked.

"I'm not in the mood to deal with Jamal right now," Brent said.

"Oh, okay," MJ said. "Sorry that you two are behaving like middle school children."

Brent cocked his eyebrow at her.

"Just admit it, MJ," Mimi said. "You want to see Jamal."

"I see I'm surrounded by adolescents today," MJ quipped. "If I wanted to see Jamal, I would've called him long before now."

Brent wanted to sprint from the table, but he could see Mimi's concern as she looked at him.

"Brent? Are you all right?"

"Long day. I'll be fine, just need to figure some things out and get out of here before Jamal shows up."

"I'll go with you." Mimi picked up her purse as Brent rose to his feet.

MJ nodded toward the front of the restaurant. "Too late."

Mimi squeezed Brent's elbow. "Are you going to be all right?" she asked.

Not if you don't move your hand. "I'm good. We're all adults here."

Jamal approached the table and shook his head. "So, this is how we're playing it now?"

"What's up, Jamal?"

"You really want to get into this now?" he asked, his voice peppered with annoyance.

"I'm getting real sick of you trying to tell me what kind of relationship I need to have with my father," Brent bellowed.

Mimi and MJ exchanged worried looks. "Guys," MJ said. "Maybe this isn't the time and place."

"When is the time, when this jackass keeps avoiding me?" Jamal snapped.

"I don't want to talk to you about my father and how I deal with him. Why does it matter so much to you?"

Jamal pinched the bridge of his nose. "I don't want to do this here," he said. "We really need to sit down and have a real conversation."

"Tell me now or forget it."

"My little brother needs to know that when y'all's father dies that he's going have someone he can depend on."

Brent held his hands up. "Why in the hell does it matter to you? And what does your little brother have to do with anything?"

"He's your brother, too."

Brent's mouth dropped open and Mimi gasped. Now it made sense; the doctor said *sons*. But Jamal's little brother?

"I'm out of here," Brent said. Jamal reached out

for his friend, but the angry look on Brent's face gave
him pause.

"What in the world just happened?" MJ whispered.

"Something that should've happened a long time
ago," Jamal said. "I'm going go find him."

"No. I'm going to talk to him." Mimi dashed out of
the restaurant.

Brent paced back and forth on the sidewalk in front
of the restaurant. How was that even possible? Brent
knew Jamal's mother, or at least he thought he did.
How could he not know that she had an affair with his
father? How could Jamal not tell him?

"Shit," he muttered.

"Brent?"

Turning around, he saw Mimi standing there.
"What's going on?" he asked as he crossed over to her.

"That's why I'm here. Are you all right?" she said,
placing her hand on his cheek.

He sighed. "I just can't wrap my mind around everything right now."

"Want to talk about it?" she asked as she leaned
against him.

"No. Mimi, I don't want to talk. Come home with
me?"

She nodded. "What happened back there with you
and Jamal?"

"I want to do a lot of things, Mimi, and talking isn't
one of them." Brent wrapped his arms around her waist
and it felt too good to hold her. The walk to the car was
torture. Her hot body against his made his libido sky-
rocket. Once he had Mimi buckled into the passenger
seat of his car, Brent got into the driver's seat. Glancing

at Mimi, he noticed that she had her eyes closed as if he was deep in thought. Beautiful. She was so beautiful. His gaze fell on her lips and he wanted to kiss her so badly. But he had to follow the rules. Starting the car, Brent knew the sooner he got Mimi home, the better he would feel. This case had to get settled soon. He needed to taste the most intimate parts of Mimi Collins, needed to get her off his mind. But what if one taste wasn't enough?

Could she be the woman he'd been waiting for? One thing was for sure—Mimi wasn't like any woman he'd ever met. She had a free spirit and didn't get caught up in the image-conscious nature of Atlanta. As much as he didn't want to think about Jamal right now, he had been right about one thing, Brent had dated women who looked good on paper. Mimi Collins was off the charts.

And he felt as if he could open up to her about one of the most difficult parts of his life. They got out of the car and walked inside the building in silence. Once they made it to her door, she looked up at him and he was overcome with so many pent-up emotions.

"Brent?"

"Yeah?"

"Tell me what's going on. I've laid my problems on you. Let me listen to you for a change."

"Just knowing that you want to be here for me means a lot." He leaned in and kissed her on the forehead. Their eyes locked. And for once, Brent didn't care about the rules. He didn't want to talk. He wanted to kiss her. And in a swift motion, he captured her lips, pulling her against his body. He ripped his mouth from hers and licked his lips.

"I need you, Mimi."

"But…"

"I need you." He stroked her cheek. "I need you."

Mimi nodded. Brent took her keys from her hand and unlocked her door. Once they were inside, Brent pressed her against the wall and kissed her slow and deep. He slipped his hand inside her shirt, massaging her breast until her nipple hardened and she moaned. He ran his tongue up and down the column of her neck.

Bringing his lips to her ear, his flicked his tongue against her lobe. "I want to make love to you, Mimi. Let me make love to you."

"Please. Please."

Brent scooped her up in his arms and headed for her bedroom. He laid her on the bed and Mimi started to take her clothes off. Brent drank in her image in black lace panties and smiled. She was more beautiful than he'd ever fantasized about.

She reached for his belt, but Brent grabbed her hand. "Just let me look at you. You're so beautiful."

He joined her on the bed and took his shirt off. Then he pulled Mimi against his chest. Feeling her skin against his made his body burn with desire. Then she found his hot spot—his left nipple—with her tongue and he couldn't wait another second to make love to her.

He was crossing a line that he'd vowed he never would, but with everything that happened tonight, he needed Mimi's tenderness, her warmth, her loving.

Pulling back from her, he quickly disrobed, then wrapped her legs around his waist. Skin to skin, lips to lips, Brent had never felt so good with a woman in his arms. Mimi's skin felt like silk. And her lips were like sugar. He wanted nothing more than to dive into her wetness, but they had to be protected. Mimi seemed to read his mind as she reached into her nightstand drawer and grabbed a condom. Brent took it from her hand, then pushed her back on the pillows. Spreading her thighs apart, he stroked her wetness, taking control of her body. She responded to his touch with vigor, her body moving as his fingers commanded.

Then Brent planted his face between her legs, licking and sucking her sweet wetness. Mimi's moans filled the air and Brent grew harder and harder. As he nibbled at her throbbing bud, all he could think about was feeling her wrapped around his hardness.

"Oh, Brent," she moaned.

Easing back from her, Brent smiled at the look of bliss on her face. "Need to be inside you." He sheathed his erection and thrust into her. They moved in a singular motion, rocking back and forth as if they were riding ocean waves.

"You feel so good."

"Brent, Brent."

"Come for me, baby." He thrust harder and deeper. She shivered in his arms as her climax took hold. Moments later, Brent exploded inside her. They fell into each other's arms and exhaled.

"Oh, my God," Mimi exclaimed. "That was amazing."

Brent smiled as he toyed with one of her curls. Yes, making love to Mimi was amazing, but they'd crossed a big line. She was still his client and as good as it felt, it was so wrong. Mimi caught the pensive look in his eyes.

"What's wrong?"

Brent exhaled. "Mimi, you know you're amazing, right. But we…"

"Don't say it. Don't start talking about rules right now, Brent."

He stroked her cheek. "We crossed the line and this can't happen again until I'm done with your case."

She expelled a sigh and shifted out of his embrace. "Brent, you are the most irritating man I've ever met! How can you lie here with me right now, after what we shared, and think about rules?"

He wanted to tell her that it was because of his father's legacy, but when she leaped from the bed and started pacing the room, he couldn't. Not when she looked so good naked and angry.

"Mimi."

"Don't *Mimi* me!"

"I can't have this conversation with you when you're naked." His lopsided smirk seemed to calm Mimi. She stopped pacing and shook her head.

"Okay." She grabbed her robe from the back of the closet and put it on. "Brent. You're not the only one who broke a rule. I don't hop into bed with a man without considering how things are going to move forward. I…"

"What?"

"Nothing."

"Babe, let it out."

"I don't want to be hurt. And I need to know that this goes beyond me being a warm body for you because of what you were going through tonight."

She walked over to the bed and Brent pulled her into his lap. "It does. This isn't a one-night stand, Mimi. And you are more than a warm body. Actually, you're pretty hot."

She playfully punched him on the shoulder. "Tell me something I don't know."

He looked into her eyes and wanted to tell her that he was falling in love with her. "Mimi."

"Don't. Since we've already broken the rules, let's just keep going."

He laughed. "What do you have against rules?"

Mimi shrugged as she sat on his lap and wrapped her arms around his neck. "I like to blaze my own path and this lawsuit has made me do things I never wanted to do."

"Like what?"

"I had to censor my blog today, and I don't like doing that."

"Have you ever thought about maybe toning it down on your blog?"

"Are we starting this again? My blog is mine and I'm going to run it as I damn well please." She dropped her arms from his neck and rose to her feet.

"Then you'd better put me on retainer. Fast Love is just the beginning. Other people are going to see this suit, no matter how it turns out, as a way to come after you and try to take you down. Or for marketing purposes. Mimi, you know that people listen to what you say and take your words to heart. Why do…"

"Stop!" she exclaimed. "Maybe you need society to give you a rubber stamp or a pat on the back so that you can feel good about yourself. I don't live like that."

"No, you hide online where you think you're untouchable, but you're not. If this lawsuit hasn't taught you that, I don't know what will."

"You know what, I think you should go. I don't want to spend another minute with a man who's too afraid to live. You're perfect for Atlanta. Image is everything for you."

"Fine." Brent dressed, then slammed out of her place.

Mimi sat alone in her bed pondering what Brent had said.

He made a good point, but it was a point she wasn't ready to accept—especially from him.

But why did it matter so much? Brent Daniels was just a man. A sexy, sensual man who had been haunting her dreams since he kissed her. A man she wanted to make love to again more than she wanted to take her next breath. But Mimi knew she could never have anything serious with Brent because she wasn't one of those women he obviously found appropriate. He thought she needed to be tamed, and she wasn't a damned horse.

Seeing Jamal waiting for him the hallway made Brent cringe. He didn't want to walk from one argument to another.

"Are you going to talk to me or what?" Jamal asked as Brent unlocked his door.

"I don't want to talk to you right now," Brent said. "Talking to you means you've lied to me for years and I don't want to accept that right now."

"I tried to tell you," Jamal said. "I wanted you to know about my mother and your father, but every time I said something about your dad, you shut me down."

"How did this happen?" Brent asked.

"I asked her to skip the details, but she was a part of the prison ministry and she met your father. Since we were friends, she'd give him updates on you."

Donna Carver used to be one of his favorite people but hearing this was changing his opinion. "And how did that lead to her sleeping with the man and getting pregnant?"

Jamal sighed. "I can't wrap my mind around that, either. One thing led to another and I was going to take it to my grave until she had Daveon."

"Ten years, though? Ten years you kept your mouth closed and now because that bastard is dying I'm supposed to step in?"

"No one is asking you to step in to do anything. Daveon is my little brother and we've done a good job of taking care of him. Unlike you, he doesn't hate his father. And it would be nice for him to know his other brother since both of you are losing your father."

Brent closed his eyes. Things were beginning to make sense. "Why didn't you just tell me?"

"And give you another reason to hate your father? And I wasn't sure how you were going to react to my mother, because friend or not, I wasn't going to allow you to disrespect her."

"I'd never disrespect your mother and just like you, I don't need the details of their affair, relationship or whatever. Is she still in contact with him?"

Jamal nodded. "She takes Daveon to see him once a month. You know what my mother has been through and how we've struggled with her addictions for years. Even after she had Daveon, she was still struggling. Gran had been raising him and it wasn't until your father got sick that she took a more active role in his life."

"You mean all of this time, my—our—little brother has been living with your grandmother?"

Jamal nodded.

"All right," Brent said. "I guess I do need to have a conversation with my dad and your mother before I meet Daveon and…"

Jamal reached out to shake Brent's hand. "Look, I hated lying to you and trying to force you into a relationship you didn't want with your dad, but…"

"You were looking out for your family and I can't fault you for that."

"You're family, too," Jamal said. "And what in the hell is going on with you and Mimi?"

Brent closed his eyes; images of making love to Mimi flashed in his head. He wasn't the guy to kiss and tell, but he was aching with the fact that he'd crossed a huge line with Mimi.

Jamal shook his head. "It's pretty obvious that she wants you as much as you want her."

"Let's just say things are pretty complicated."

"That's because you're making things that way. Go get that woman."

Brent shook his head. He couldn't be next to Mimi's heat right now.

Chapter 14

Mimi woke up to the sound of her phone ringing. She tried to ignore the throbbing in her head. All she needed was five minutes. A snooze button. But someone wanted to talk to her this morning.

Reaching for her phone, she hoped that it was MJ with good news. "Hello," she breathed.

"Mimi?" an unfamiliar voice asked.

"Yes, and you are?"

"Kayla White from Del-Ray Publishing. I'm Kita Jameson's assistant."

"Oh, good morning."

"Kita wants to speak with you."

Mimi sat up in her bed. She couldn't remember the last time she had a one-on-one conversation with her editor. "Great," she said, forcing the sleep from her voice.

"Mimi, good morning," Kita said. "What's going on with your blog?"

"What do you mean?"

"Usually there's fresher content, more page views. I know you have this thing with Fast Love going on right now, but…"

"Wait, I just put a piece up yesterday."

"Yes, and it was so tame," Kita said with a sigh. "A travel piece about a city you want to visit. It just didn't have the punch that your blog posts normally have. Do you have someone representing you in this case? I could talk to the…"

"Kita, I have a lawyer. But what do you mean about the punch of my blog? Is that what you're looking for in my book?"

"Duh. Haven't you and MJ been talking about the plan for the Mis-Adventures of Mimi Collins brand? We have to capitalize on the success of your first book."

"I love how y'all are having these discussions without me."

"Mimi, you are on your way to being a superstar. We're just trying to make that happen for you."

"I'm going to need a say in that," Mimi snapped. "And I'd like to talk to you about my next book. When is that going to happen?"

"As soon as your blog starts breaking the internet again. Mimi, I think you're a great writer. But you have to know this is a business and needs to be treated as such. MJ told me about your desire to do something different with your book. We're not ready to go that route yet. People are going to want the magic of your blog in book form. That's…"

"All right," Mimi said. "Whatever."

"But we don't want to proceed with this lawsuit hanging over your head. Are you sure you don't want me to sic some of our lawyers on Fast Love?"

"Sure you don't want to use this for marketing?" Mimi muttered.

"That's not a bad idea, even though I know you're being sarcastic. And that is what we're missing from the blog right now. Why don't you put that back in your next post?"

"Bye, Kita." After hanging up, Mimi pulled herself out of bed and headed to the kitchen for a huge glass of water. Her head throbbed from the conversation with her editor. Maybe she didn't need the book deal, especially if she was going to be forced to write things for marketing purposes. Groaning, Mimi started her coffee machine. She needed a jolt before she got to work and apologized to Brent for her behavior last night. Yes, she had a right to be upset, but he was only trying to help her. He didn't have to take her case, but he did. Mimi knew she needed to start taking his advice seriously. Especially if she wanted to win this case. Fast Love needed to learn a lesson.

Once the coffee was brewed, Mimi filled two mugs, then headed across the hall to Brent's door.

Brent had just hung up with his secretary, telling her that he wouldn't be in until noon. He needed the morning to wrap his mind around what Jamal had shared with him last night.

Daveon was his brother. Donna had fallen for his father when she should have run away from him like nylons on a rosebush. He picked up his phone to call the prison doctor. It was time to take his mother's advice and get closure with his father. As he was about to dial the number, there was a knock at his door. Placing the phone on the coffee table, he crossed the room and looked out of the peephole. He saw Mimi standing on the other side of the door with two mugs in her hands.

Opening the door, he leaned against the doorjamb and gave her a cool once-over. No one should be that sexy in a T-shirt and cotton shorts. Then he made the mistake of looking down at her toes. The purple polish made him think of candy, which made him yearn to suck her toes.

"Mmm, good morning," she said. "I know you probably, and rightfully so, don't want to talk to me right now. But I wanted to say I was sorry for my behavior last night and offer you some Dancing Goats coffee."

Brent had planned to give her the cold shoulder, brush her off and ignore her apology. But did she just say *Dancing Goats coffee?*

"Dancing Goats coffee? Should I be afraid?" he asked with a laugh.

"No, Dancing Goats is the most amazing coffee in Atlanta. The world, actually. I thought my apology might be accepted better if you took a sip." She held a mug out to him.

"It's not made from goat nuggets, is it?" he asked as he took the mug.

"No! It's Ethiopian. Legend says, a farmer found the beans after his goats ate some and started dancing around the field. Hence, the name. It's really good and I'm really sorry about last night."

Brent took a sip of the coffee and Mimi had been right. It was delicious. "Wow," he said. "This is good. Almost good enough to make me forget last night."

Mimi rolled her eyes. "Perhaps you need another sip."

"Come in so that we can talk in private," he said. Mimi smiled.

"I was wondering if this was going to happen," she muttered.

"I thought about leaving you standing out there," he replied, silently adding, *But I wanted to get an up close and personal look at those legs.* Brent led Mimi into the living room and invited her to sit on the sofa. He sat across from her in his leather recliner. Brent watched her as she fluidly crossed her legs and sipped her coffee. He was hard. And he felt as if this was the first time his erection had sapped his brainpower. Focusing on his mug, Brent cleared his throat. "So, Mimi, what are we doing?" he asked.

She set her mug on the table in front of her. "Brent, I've been a jerk. Or an asshole depending on how you look at it. When I started my blog, I could count on one hand the people who supported me. So when anyone, you or my editor, try to tell me what I should be writing about, it pisses me off."

"Why the anger? Why let it consume you? All of those people who thought you couldn't do it have been proven wrong."

"Have they? Brent," Mimi said with a sigh, "I feel like I'm stuck in a rut."

"Really? You have a popular blog. Everyone in Atlanta loves what you do from what I can tell."

"I want more than that. Haven't you ever thought about trying a case in front of the Supreme Court?"

"It's okay to be satisfied," he said. "And I am."

Mimi sighed again. She sipped her coffee to hold

back her disappointment. Of course he loved Atlanta. How could he not be satisfied here? Another reason why they couldn't be together.

"What?" he asked when he caught the pensive look in her eye.

Mimi shrugged and set her coffee mug on the table. "Nothing. I'm just thinking about everything and nothing. Anyway, how's the coffee?"

"It's everything you said it was," he said with a wink.

"You should visit the café and get one of their designer lattes. Pretty and delicious."

"Like you," he said, then immediately regretted it.

"You need to stop teasing me," she said as she crossed her legs. Brent looked at her strong thighs and the thoughts that ran through his mind were nearly too erotic for words. He wanted to be in between those thighs, tasting the sweetness of her core. Wanted those thighs resting on his shoulders as his tongue teased and licked her until she screamed his name.

"Brent?"

He blinked and looked up at her face. "Yeah?"

"Are you and Jamal all right? I know I was in my own world last night, but I could tell y'all were having an issue."

"It's a long and twisted story. His mother and my father have a son together."

Blinking, Mimi couldn't come up with a single thing to say. Brent nodded as she stumbled for words. "I know. My parents have been divorced for a long time and he's been in prison for a while. I had no idea that Jamal's mother had a relationship or an affair with him.

Now I have to deal with that, get to know my little brother and make peace with my dad before he dies."

"Wow, and I'm upset about a blog," she said. "I'm truly sorry for acting like a witch last night when you have all of this going on." Mimi crossed over to him and in a move that caught him off guard, she planted herself on his lap and gave him a tight hug. Brent had to shift his hips or she would've felt the immediate effect she had on him. "You're going through a lot and you're still helping me. You're a saint, Brent," she said, then rose to her feet.

Brent stood up and stroked Mimi's shoulder. He wanted this woman as much as he needed his next breath. "I'm no saint, but thank you. As a matter of fact, I have an idea that might get this Fast Love situation taken care of sooner rather than later. Thanks for the coffee," he said as he smiled at her.

"My publisher offered to represent me in this case and if you need to step aside because of your family situation, I'm fine with that."

Looking her up and down, Brent knew he should take the out because he wanted to scoop her up in his arms and take her to bed. "I'm not walking away from this case, not when we're about to win."

"You sure don't lack confidence," she said.

"Why should I? No one can do what I do," he said with a wink. Mimi shivered at the thought of the double entendre.

"You are right about that. Your skills are very amazing."

"It's what I do," he said as they walked to the door. After Mimi left, Brent called Judith.

"Brent," she said when she answered the phone. "I

was waiting for your call. I have a meeting with the CEO and marketing director of Fast Love in about two hours. I think they are willing to drop the claim against Mimi Collins."

"I guess her millions of followers on social media changed their minds, huh?" Brent said with a chuckle. "I look forward to hearing their decision."

"I'll call you as soon as I know," she said, then the call was disconnected.

Brent wanted to rush over to Mimi and tell her the news, but there was no need to get her hopes up if things didn't work in their direction. Besides, he couldn't allow this to stop him from going to see his father, even if part of him wanted to do just that. Heading into the bathroom, he took a shower and prepared himself to meet with a man he said he'd never speak to again.

Mimi stood at the kitchen counter and poured another cup of coffee. She wanted to sip on Brent again, not her favorite brew. But if he started talking about rules and lines again, she was going to lose her mind.

"Get it together, Mimi," she muttered as she took a sip of the steaming brew. There were fifty things she could be doing right now rather than obsessing over Brent Daniels. She needed to post a blog. Crossing over to her workspace, Mimi sat down at the computer and her mind went totally blank. Then she decided to do some maintenance on the blog. She couldn't help herself from looking at the page views of her blog about New Orleans. Ten thousand. Less than any other post she'd written in the last twenty days.

That wasn't good. Especially when the Fast Love

post was still racking up views. Hell, it was the most read piece on her blog ever.

"Fast Love, I hope you go out of business," she muttered as she clicked her browser closed. Forget writing, she was going to take a run and pretend she didn't feel melancholy about people only wanting to read her posts about relationship drama. And it wasn't as if she was in a relationship! Or wanted to be in one—well, could have the one she wanted. Brent was back in the forefront of her mind.

This wasn't supposed to happen. He'd already told her that he was satisfied with his life in Atlanta. That wasn't going to work for her.

Deciding that she wasn't going to get anything done, she called MJ. Voice mail. That was strange—that girl kept her cell phone in her hand as if it was glued there.

Run. Mimi was going to take a run and hopefully clear her mind. After dressing in her workout gear, she headed out and noticed Brent leaving as well. His attire, jeans and a T-shirt surprised her. Obviously he wasn't going to the office.

"Yes," she heard him say into the phone as he walked. "I'm on my way. It shouldn't take long."

Was he taking the day off to spend it with some woman after he had been with her? Why was she jealous and why did she care? Mimi took off running in the opposite direction hoping that he didn't see her. Maybe the reason why he'd rebuffed her had little to do with her being his client and more to do with the woman in his life.

As she ran, she got angrier. So, he was one of those typical Atlanta men, flirting and kissing other women but had a boo out in Sandy Springs. Jackass. Looking up, Mimi realized that she'd run about two miles. Stopping, she bent over and held her knees. Why was she doing this to herself?

Mimi walked back to her home, still cursing Brent out in her head. This wasn't how her day was supposed to go. Retail therapy. Some new shoes or a nice lacy bra would be just what she needed.

When she got inside, she grabbed her cell phone and dialed MJ's number again.

Voice mail.

"MJ, what's going on with you? Call me!" Mimi said, then hung up the phone. Heading upstairs to hop in the shower, Mimi figured she needed to be alone.

Chapter 15

Brent drummed his fingers on the metal table as he waited for his father. Sitting in a waiting room in a prison wasn't new for hm. He sat in rooms like this to meet with clients on a regular basis. But today was different. He didn't want to be here. He had to be here.

As he heard the door open, he watched the guard lead his father inside and was shocked by what he saw. Brent Sr. was gaunt. A shell of his former self. His face was sunken and his once-massive arms looked like sticks.

"Hello, son," Brent Sr. said, his voice hoarse and raspy as he sat down.

"Dad." Brent made no effort to embrace the man at all. Instead, he leaned away from him in his seat, folding his arms across his chest.

"It's really good to see you," Brent Sr. said, then coughed.

"So, you're dying?"

He nodded. "And you're still angry with me."

"Why wouldn't I be? You made my life and my mother's life a living hell. I'm supposed to feel sorry for you now? We lost everything. We lost our house. People wouldn't even talk to us because of you."

"No. You shouldn't. But I want to make things right before I die. I did horrible things. I'm surprised you actually came back to Atlanta after you finished law school."

"It sure wasn't easy, being your son and all."

"I let greed and power get to me. This cancer is my penance, not the jail sentence. I wasn't a good father and I'm sorry. I wanted you to be strong and nothing like me."

"It worked. The only thing we share is a name."

Brent Sr. dropped his head. "Can you let me apologize?"

"Go ahead," he replied.

"I found peace in here. I've been humbled and I've changed. I thought I'd have a chance to get things right and treat my sons better."

Brent's jaw went rigid. "And," Brent Sr. continued, "I fell in love again."

"Yeah, with my best friend's mother. How in the hell did that happen?"

"I didn't know who she was at first. Donna was just a beautiful lady who brought me the good word. She touched my heart and one thing led to another. I have a confession. We were married two weeks ago. I wanted to make sure she and Daveon will be taken care of when I pass on. And there's something I need you to help me with."

Brent smirked. "I should've known this was more than you trying to make things right between us. Of course you need something."

Brent Sr. started coughing again. His bony shoulders shook violently. Brent wanted to reach out to him, but a mixture of fear and anger kept him rooted in his seat.

When the older man caught his breath, he focused his glassy stare on his son. "Can you draw up my will? I need my family to be taken care of when I die. Daveon is innocent. I didn't ruin him. Please."

Though the little boy inside him felt a sharp flash of jealousy, Brent remembered what his mother said about closure. And his father was right. Daveon was innocent and he deserved to be taken care of because he didn't ask to come into this crazy world.

"All right," Brent said. "I'll get it done by the end of the day."

Brent Sr. pulled a handwritten will from the back pocket of his uniform and handed it to his son. "These are the stipulations," he said. "Thank you, son."

Brent stood up and nodded at his father. "You have changed, for the better. I wish I had more time to get to know this man."

Brent Sr. rose to his feet and reached out for Brent's hand. After a beat, Brent took his father's hand and then the men hugged.

"I'm so sorry," Brent Sr. mumbled as his tears spilled onto Brent's shoulder. "Even if you don't forgive me, please don't let your little brother not know you."

Stepping back from his father, Brent nodded. "Okay. I'll get to know him and take care of the will."

The guard opened the door. "Time's up," he growled. Watching his father being led away, Brent finally felt something other than anger. For the first time, he was sad that he might never see his father again.

Mimi stood in the middle of her favorite lingerie store with a handful of black and red lace panties and bras. Part of her wanted to put everything back. Who was going to see these things?

Maybe I should write a blog about why women should stockpile lingerie for themselves, Mimi thought as she picked up a leopard-print teddy. With the right shoes, she would knock Brent dead in this outfit. Why was she even entertaining dressing sexy for that cheater?

"Miss Collins?" Porsha, her sales associate, said. "Are you ready to check out?"

"Yes," Mimi replied with a smile. Porsha had been her go-to girl since Sexy Secrets opened in midtown. It helped that Porsha was a reader of her blog.

"Hot date or are you packing for New Orleans? You blog made me want to head to the French Quarter immediately."

"You read that and liked it?" Mimi didn't even try to keep the surprise out of her voice.

"Yes, you know I love your writing. I could totally see you in New Orleans. You'd turn that city upside down and probably find some sexy Creole man while you're there. I can't wait to read about it. And when is the new book coming out?"

Mimi groaned inwardly. "Soon. I have to get some legal stuff cleared up first."

"I can't believe Fast Love is suing you. But your attorney is so fine! How can you stand it? I'd love to see his legal briefs."

"I'm sure someone is looking at them right now," Mimi mumbled. Thankfully, Porsha didn't hear her as they walked toward the register. After paying for her items, Mimi decided that she deserved something chocolate and delicious. Since she couldn't have Brent, she'd settle for a sinfully rich slice of chocolate cheesecake from Sweet Hut.

As she climbed into her car, Mimi made a decision. She was going to move to New Orleans at the end of the month. She was going to write her travel book, even if she had to publish it herself. She'd give the publisher the relationship book they wanted and she was going to post her blog about kissing Brent. After all, who would know that it was about him, anyway?

Feeling at ease, Mimi was happy to make her stop at the bakery. She wasn't even going to call MJ back, because she needed to wallow in her disappointment alone.

Brent headed to Jamal's house with the will he'd drawn up. He was actually happy to share the news about his father with his friend. For a change, this probably wouldn't lead to an argument. When he pulled into the driveway, he noticed a strange car parked behind Jamal's.

That was different, because he didn't usually bring women home, not since the Mina Clarke incident. Brent chuckled as he thought about the woman who'd toilet-papered Jamal's front yard and left dead fish in his mailbox after he stopped returning her calls.

He'd sworn off sharing his address with a woman unless he was serious about her. And since Jamal had no plans to get serious with anyone, this car must have belonged to his mother. Brent parked at the curb and headed for the front steps. When the door opened and MJ walked out, Brent was shocked. Then they kissed and Brent nearly fell on his face.

"Wow," he said. The startled couple turned around and gave him a guilty look.

"Umm, I have to go," MJ said as she brushed past Brent.

"What are you doing here?" Jamal asked when MJ slammed her car door. "I thought you were going to see your father."

"I did. That's why I'm here. But the bigger question is what's up with you and MJ?"

Jamal grinned. "You know I never kiss and tell."

"Since when, King of TMI?"

"MJ is special. I haven't met a woman like her ever," Jamal said. Brent would've laughed and pointed out to his friend that MJ was the kind of woman he usually ran from, but he just listened to him.

"She's driven and wants to be her own woman, not just *the wife of* or some reality star vixen."

"That's rare to find these days," Brent said. His mind immediately flipped to Mimi. She was a woman like no other and he was falling hard and fast for her.

"Did you see your father?"

"I did. We actually came to an understanding."

Jamal took a step back. "Wow. That's great."

"He's changed. I imagine prison does that to a man."

"Not only that, but he knows he doesn't have much time left. I'm sure he wants to make these last moments in his life count. Brent, I know you had a different relationship with your father, but he wanted to be a better man for Daveon."

"I know. He's made sure Daveon will be taken care of for the rest of his life. He's the beneficiary of our father's life insurance policy. I just drew up his final will. Your mother's love changed my father and I'm glad I got a chance to see it. Doesn't make my past with him any better, but it's good to know he learned some lessons."

"You don't resent his relationship with my brother?" Jamal asked. "I mean, I could understand if you did…"

"Daveon didn't do anything wrong and neither did your mother. My issues with my father don't include them, or you for that matter. I'm going to take a page from my mother's book and move on."

"And what are you going to do about Mimi?"

As if on cue, Brent's cell phone rang. He looked down at the screen and saw it was Fast Love's attorney calling.

"I have to take this," he said. "This is Brent."

"Brent, Judith here. I have some news for you and Miss Collins. We're going to withdraw the complaint against the website."

Brent pumped his fist, glad Judith couldn't see his excitement. "That's a very good decision on your part. I will inform Miss Collins of your decision.

"I'm sure you will. We actually found that there was a problem in the marketing of the event and we've acknowledged the mistake in a statement on Fast Love's website. Tell Miss Collins that we apologize for the inconvenience and we hope that we can work together in the future," Judith said.

"Sure thing," Brent said, then disconnected the call. He turned to Jamal with a smile on his face. "I have to go."

"Good news for Miss Collins, I assume."

"And me, too," Brent said, then dashed to his car.

Mimi ignored the rantings of her editor. Fresh content, more page views on the blog. They'd just had this conversation less than eight hours ago. "Mimi," Kita said, "you're making it hard for the marketing department to push the book. The numbers have to come up on your blog. These little puff pieces aren't cutting it."

"I'm trying to..." Mimi's phone buzzed indicating that she had a text message. "Kita, that's my lawyer. I need to call you back." Brent's text was a welcome distraction from her editor's pressure. Yes, the numbers had dropped because Mimi had rerun some of her more popular pieces, and she had written another travel piece about New York. Hell, when she posted that one she'd known it was cliché as hell. Everybody has been to New York.

Fast Love gave up. We need to celebrate. And, I quit.

Mimi rolled her eyes. Celebrate? Was he serious? He may have worked his legal magic to get the case tossed aside, but she wasn't going to be his booty call. Mimi sighed with relief and frustration. Now that this thing was over, she could write what she wanted to again. Maybe she would post her blog about Brent. Kita would be happy, the numbers would go up, and her book deal would be saved.

Looking at her phone, she sent Brent the text reply she hated most.

K

Brent replied immediately. Are you busy or something? Expected a lot more enthusiasm. Chocolate or sushi?

Mimi wasn't going to turn down free food, and maybe confronting him over sushi would make things easier.

Sushi is great, and sake.

No sake.

Plenty of sake!

How about plenty of kisses?

Mimi dropped her phone. No matter how much she drank, she wasn't going to kiss him. She wasn't going to fall for his slick talk and sexy eyes. Turning back to her laptop, Mimi decided to write about the end of her suit with Fast Love. Just as she was about to publish her blog, the phone rang.

"It's about time you returned a call, MJ," Mimi said when she answered.

"I'm in trouble."

"What? Where are you? What's going on?" Mimi turned away from her laptop.

"I think I'm falling for Jamal."

"Girl!" Mimi sucked her teeth. "I was ready to get Vaseline ready and head... Wait, are you insane?"

"Spending time with Jamal has been so refreshing and he's different."

"He's a player just like his friend. At least he's honest about it."

"Are you talking about Brent? He actually caught us today."

Mimi rolled her eyes even though her friend couldn't see her. "You guys aren't the only ones who got busted today."

"What do you mean?"

"Brent obviously has a woman out in the burbs somewhere. I heard him on the phone when I was going for a run."

"You're always jumping to conclusions. He went to see his father today. Jamal was nervous and we talked about it this afternoon."

Mimi felt like a real jackass. "Oh, my God."

"Yeah. According to Jamal this was a big step for him, given his relationship with his father."

Mimi groaned. "I'm such an asshole."

"I don't disagree with you there," MJ said. "What's the deal with you guys?"

"Well, he got the Fast Love matter solved and he said he wanted to celebrate."

"He doesn't work for you anymore, so now you can…"

"I've got to go, MJ," Mimi said as she looked down at her tank top and boxer shorts.

"But wait! I need you to talk me off the ledge. I can't fall for Jamal."

"Can I write about it on my blog?"

"No!"

"Then we can talk about it later."

"You know this is all your fault with your 'rebounding is okay' mess," MJ said. "Let's do lunch tomorrow."

"Sure, and don't put this on me, because you said you didn't read my blog."

"Okay," MJ said. After Mimi hung up, she dashed to the bathroom for a shower.

Brent pulled his phone from his pocket and waited for Mimi to text him back. He'd wanted her lips pressed against his for a long time. His hunger for her had been nearly overwhelming. That's why there would be no sake tonight. He wanted to get drunk on Mimi. He started to text her again, but since he knew where she lived, he'd just knock on her door with the sushi and roses. He just had to find flowers that matched Mimi: red, yellow and orange. Fiery and beautiful. As he crossed the street heading toward the florist shop, his cell phone rang.

"This is Brent," he said when he answered the call.

"Mr. Daniels," a woman's voice said.

"Who am I speaking with?"

"Nasheka Samuels from the Department of Corrections."

"Is this about my father?" A cold feeling of dread settled in the pit of his stomach.

"Yes, he has been taken to the hospital. We think he had a stroke and he's going to need to be tested by doctors other than our prison doctors."

"What do I need to do?" he asked, feeling helpless. This wasn't supposed to happen today.

"At this time," she began, "we think your father may not make it. If you have family members who want to see him, you should get with them now."

"What hospital will he be going to?" Brent knew he had to go and see his father for the last time. And though he wanted to meet Daveon—he'd hoped it would be under better circumstances—he had to tell him and his mother to come to the hospital. Nasheka gave him the directions to the hospital, then Brent sent Jamal a text.

Speeding to the hospital, Brent prayed that he wasn't too late to say goodbye.

Chapter 16

Mimi was not a patient woman. Waiting for Brent was driving her crazy. She started to call him, but she didn't want to come off as being overly anxious. But damn it, she was hungry. Checking her phone, it had been two hours since Brent's text about kisses. Maybe he'd gotten a better offer. *Or maybe something happened with his family. Why do I keep looking for something bad to happen?* Mimi tossed back and forth in her living room, ignoring the doubts in her mind. Brent was going to show up and they would have a talk. She'd apologize and get her kisses—and maybe something else.

She looked up at the clock above her TV and sighed. He obviously wasn't going to celebrate with her tonight. Mimi crossed over to her laptop and reread the blog she'd written about her kiss with Brent. Reading it for a third time, she decided to post it. After she posted it, Mimi stripped off her lacy black gown and put on a pair of Atlanta Falcons sweatpants and a cropped tank top with her blog logo on it.

Mimi wiped her eyes with her fingers and then headed into the kitchen to pour herself a bowl of cereal. As soon as she dipped her spoon in the bowl, there was a knock at her door. Part of her wanted to ignore the knock. She knew Brent was on the other side of the door, and he'd kept her waiting. Wanting. Needing his lips, his touch. Anger be damned, Mimi dropped her spoon and crossed over to the door. Seeing Brent standing there with a dozen roses and a smile made her forget her irrational anger.

"I'm sorry I'm late," he said. "And that there's no sushi." Brent took a step forward. "My father died tonight."

Mimi wrapped her arms around him and felt smaller than a baby ant. "I'm sorry. If you need to be with your family…"

"I'm where I need to be. Mimi, I went to the hospital and I saw how my little brother cried and hugged him. I knew the father that I'd known was dead. Had been dead for a long time."

"Brent," she whispered.

"It's okay," he said. "I'm glad that man is gone, so when he took his last breath tonight, I felt at peace."

"Wow," she said. "Are you sure you're all right? If you need to…"

"Mimi, I've been thinking about last night for most of the day."

"Brent…"

"Just so we're clear," he began, "I want you. I want

to kiss you, I want to make love to you. I want you to scream my name so all the neighbors can hear."

Mimi's mouth formed a shape of an *O* as their eyes locked. "Are you ready?" he asked.

"I-I...yes." Before she could say anything else, Brent captured her sexy mouth in a heated kiss. Mimi melted in his arms as his tongue tangled with hers. Mimi's mouth was ripe for the taking and Brent was determined to take it all. Her soft moans spurred him to deepen the kiss, drop the roses and cup her backside. He pulled her so close to his body that he felt her beating heart. Mimi's heat made him harder than granite stones. Though he wanted to rip her sweatpants and tank top off, Brent knew he had to take his time. He wanted to savor every inch of her, every part of her. Scooping her up in his arms, he headed for the bedroom.

Mimi's body shivered as Brent crossed the threshold of her bedroom.

He pulled her top over her head, exposing her supple breasts. His mouth watered at the sight of her hard nipples and he leaned in to take one of the chocolate drops in his mouth. Kicking out of her sweatpants, Mimi pressed her body against his mouth and cried out in pleasure as his fingers grazed her other nipple. He slipped his free hand between her thighs, seeking her wetness as his lips closed around her neck. As he licked her up and down her regal column, Brent slipped his finger inside her womanly core, seeking her throbbing bud.

Mimi screamed in delight as he made small circles inside her with his fingertip. Her desire poured like a summer rainstorm. Pulling his finger out of her, Brent smiled at Mimi.

"I have to taste your sweetness," he murmured and then dipped his head between her thighs. The sensations his tongue sent down Mimi's spine as he licked and sucked her sweet bud were incredible.

"Brent! Brent! Brent!" she screamed. Her body shook as the waves of her orgasm washed over her love-starved body. Her dreams had nothing on the real thing. Mimi closed her eyes tighter as Brent's oral assault continued, alternating between licking and sucking.

"Look at me," he commanded gently. "Tell me how you feel."

"I-I feel good," she moaned as they locked eyes.

"Come for me, one more time," he gritted, then dived between her legs. Mimi arched her back and pressed herself against his lips. It didn't take long for her to be dripping again and shivering from an orgasm. The look of bliss on her face made Brent want her more than he needed his next breath. He made quick work of stripping out of his clothes. Mimi's eyes roamed his body, from his six-pack abs to his powerful thighs, finally settling on his erection—big, long and ready.

Mimi exhaled as she inched toward the edge of the bed. She wrapped her arms around his waist. "My turn," she said, then took his hardness into her hot mouth. Brent's knees went weak as Mimi took him deeper and deeper inside her wet mouth. Tossing his head back, he buried his hands in her cotton-soft hair. But the deeper she took him in her mouth, the harder it was for him to hold back his climax. She was magical with her lips and tongue. Brent's head rolled back as she took him deeper and deeper. When he felt his explosion coming, he pulled back. "I have to be inside you," Brent said.

"I need you inside me, now," she moaned.

"Protection," he gritted, though he would've loved to feel her hot wetness against him without a condom. Did he even have a condom?

Mimi reached into her nightstand drawer and handed him a golden package. Brent smiled. "Girl Scout?"

"Well, I'm always prepared," she replied with a grin. She watched in rapt attention as Brent slid the sheath in place. She felt herself getting wetter and wetter, ready to feel him deep inside her. Mimi inched closer to him, opening her thighs, letting him know that she was ready and waiting for his passion. Brent placed his hot hands on her thighs. Gently, he stroked her sensitive skin before wrapping her legs around his waist. "Mimi," he moaned as he dipped into her wetness.

"Yes," she cried as she threw her head back in pleasure. Brent thrust deeper and deeper into her as she clutched his back. "Deeper," she moaned as she tightened her legs around his waist. Mimi ground against his hardness, wanting to feel every inch of him. Brent pressed deeper and deeper, reveling in Mimi's wetness. Hungry for her, Brent leaned closer to her and captured her lips in a hot kiss. The combination of Mimi's tongue and the warmth of her womanly core nearly sent him over the edge. But Brent held back his orgasm as he felt the budding climax Mimi was about to experience. She was so hot and so wet.

"Come for me, baby," he groaned as he held on to his explosion. But as she tightened her walls against him, Brent could not hold back anymore. He released himself at the same time that Mimi screamed his name.

Collapsing in each other's arms, Mimi exhaled and closed her eyes. Her body was a tumble of nerves and when Brent ran his finger down her spine, she thought she was going to burst into flames. She'd waited for this for so long. Wanted to be wrapped in his embrace for so long, and the reality was much better than the dreams she'd had about this moment.

"Wow," she breathed against his chest. "Brent."

"Woman,," he said. "Whew, I'm breathless."

"So, does this mean if I ever get sued again that I need to find a new attorney?"

"Yes." Brent kissed her on the forehead. He held her closer. "Mimi."

"Yes?"

"You're amazing."

"Takes one to know one," she replied. "I've never…"

Brent covered her mouth with his as his erection sprang to life again. He needed another taste of Mimi and she was happy to oblige as she threw her leg around his waist. For the rest of the night they made love.

Mimi woke with a start as she felt Brent's arm tighten around her waist. It felt so good being wrapped up in his arms. The warmth of his breath made her tingle. She inched closer to him and was treated to the feel of his arousal.

"Good morning," he breathed against her neck. "I was wondering how much longer I'd have to wait for you to wake up."

"I see you're up and ready," she said, then pressed

her bottom closer to his erection. Brent palmed her breasts as he kissed her on the neck.

"Umm, this is the best part of waking up," he said, then licked the column of her neck. Mimi moaned as she arched her back. She was hot, wet and ready for all of Brent. Tongue. Lips. Hardness. When she felt his fingers on her thighs, Mimi shivered with hot desire. He flicked his tongue against her earlobe. She moaned. "Brent."

"So wet," he whispered as he dipped his finger inside her. Mimi screamed when the pad of his fingertip touched her clitoris.

"Brent!"

"Mimi, I need you," he breathed against her ear. "Want you."

"Take me. I'm yours."

Brent had been glad he noticed where Mimi had tucked a few extra condoms underneath her pillow because he wasn't sure if he had the willpower to be responsible and protect them. Rolling the sheath in place with one hand, he took his other hand and pulled Mimi against her hardness. Slowly, he thrust in and out of her awaiting body.

Her soft round bottom was a sight to behold as she bounced up and down with each thrust. Shifting his hips, Brent pulled Mimi on top of him.

"Ride me," he commanded.

She gripped his shoulders and tightened her thighs around him and ground against him. Slow. Deep. Wetter. Wetter. Mimi threw her head back, her breasts jutting forward, and Brent reached up to stroke her globes.

His touch sent Mimi into overdrive. She thrust

harder; her body was filled with sensations that built her explosion.

Brent, though on the brink of his own climax, wanted and needed to hear her call his name. Thrusting forward, he finally heard her breathless scream. "Brent, Brent, Brent!"

Finally, he gave in to the pleasure of her wetness and exploded. Mimi collapsed against his chest. He felt their hearts start to beat in sync as they began to bask in the afterglow.

"Never work a case for me again as long as you live," she said.

"How about you don't get sued again and I will never work for you again," he said, then kissed her forehead.

"I make no promises. After all, people are interested in what I have to say," she said then snuggled closer to him. Then as if a bucket of ice had been poured on her, Mimi shivered. Her latest blog, the blog she'd posted in anger, was all about Brent and it was live. She'd done it again.

"What's wrong?" Brent asked. "Do you have another lawsuit looming? Remember, I quit."

"No," she said, looking into his eyes. "No pending litigation. I was just thinking about all of my deadlines. The book, the blog." Inwardly she shuddered. Maybe she'd catch a break. Brent wasn't a regular reader of her blog and since the case was over, he probably wouldn't give it a second look.

She sighed and closed her eyes. Brent stroked her arm. "Is this your not-so-subtle way of telling me to get out?"

"Not at all," she said, then gently smacked his chest.

"I'd love to lie here with you all day and forget about all of my adult problems. But I'm sure you have a court case and a person to save this morning."

Brent glanced at the clock on Mimi's nightstand. It was three minutes after seven. As much as he wished he could spend the day inside Mimi, he did have a court date. Groaning, Brent shifted in bed. "You've been going through my calendar, huh?"

"No, but you are Brent Daniels, Atlanta's most wise legal mind," she said, then kissed his nipple. "People need you."

"But I need you," he said as he placed her hand on his growing erection.

"Here I am," she said as she spread her legs.

Hours later, Mimi was listening to Brent in the shower while trying to take a look at her blog. Much to her dismay, the blog about her kiss with Brent had thousands of views and just as many comments.

"Damn it," she muttered as she heard the water shut off. Mimi closed her iPad and took a deep breath. Maybe she could explain it to him. Or, she prayed, he wouldn't see it. She climbed out of bed as the door to the bathroom opened.

"My showerhead does none of the magical stuff that yours does," Brent said as he stood in the middle of Mimi's bedroom. "A few more minutes and I might have been trying to reschedule court appearances."

"That showerhead can't be that amazing," she said as she closed the space between them. Brent's fresh scent filled her nostrils and made her want to rip his towel away and keep him wrapped up in her arms all day. Then she could explain to a sated Brent why she published that blog. As she looked up at his smiling face, Mimi figured that it wouldn't be such a big deal,

He might even be flattered.

"All right, Mimi," he said as he reached for his discarded slacks. "I have to go. What do you say we meet for dinner around seven? I owe you sushi."

"And sake," she said with a grin.

"There you go with that sake talk. I've seen what sake does to you and I think we'll stick to sweet tea."

"Whatever," she said, then planted a kiss on his cheek. "We could always skip dinner and go straight for dessert."

"I like the way you think, Mimi," Brent said, then captured her lips in a hot kiss that left her breathless. When he pulled back from her, Mimi licked her bottom lip. That man was so sweet.

"You'd better go before…"

"Yeah, I know," he said with a wink. "I can't wait for tonight."

"Me either."

She walked Brent to the door and drank in his image, his shirt open and chest glistening with a few beads of water. His pants hanging low on his hips. Much better than her dreams had ever been. She just wondered if this was going to be the last time.

Chapter 17

It was only nine forty-five and Brent was having a great day. His case was dismissed and his client wouldn't have to pay a dime to the complainant. Now as he headed back to the office, he was sure that he'd wrap up his day early and head over to Mimi's for some early dessert and maybe some dinner.

He'd definitely feast on her. All day he thought about how her body felt against his, how sweet her lips and tongue were. It's a good thing he didn't have to appear in front a judge for a substantial amount of time today. He would've lost his case for sure. Mimi Collins was more than he'd ever dreamed she could be. More woman than he'd ever expected. Hell, she was the last kind of woman he expected would carve a place in his heart. But she was just what he needed. A breath of fresh air, a woman who could hold her own and didn't need a man to complete her.

Mimi was nothing like any woman he'd ever dated and that was a good thing. He owed Jamal an apology, because he'd been right. Brent had dated as if he'd been holding auditions for perfection when he should've been looking for happiness. Who knew he'd find it across the hall in a woman who was everything he thought he didn't need or want. Now he couldn't imagine being without her.

Walking into his office, Brent smiled at Rocky as he passed her desk. Was she smirking at him and giggling? Brent brushed it off. He knew his receptionist was always online looking at something borderline inappropriate.

Crossing through a group of paralegals, he stopped and listened to their hushed conversation. "She can't be talking about *him*," one said.

"Please, Mr. Law and Order is not Jesse L. Martin. It has to be Brent."

One of the paralegals looked up and locked eyes with Brent. "Oh shit," she said.

All of the women focused on their boss. "What's going on here?" Brent asked.

"Nothing," they said in unison. Then, like roaches when a bright light hit them, they all scattered. Brent crossed over to the computer they'd been huddled around and saw they were reading Mimi's blog.

He gave the page a cursory glance and when he saw *Mr. Law & Order* and *he's my neighbor*, Brent was livid. Stalking into his office, he pulled up Mimi's site and read the blog post. On one hand, he could've been flattered, but the implication of her post made it seem as if something was going on while he represented her. Brent knew he didn't have to admit the post was about him, but why would she share something so intimate online? Brent read the post again—so a relationship wasn't her thing? Then what in the hell was last night and this morning about? What were they doing? Brent knew he shouldn't have, but he started reading the comments.

Maybe he's gay, someone wrote.

Brent shook his head.

Mimi, why are you trying to ruin a relationship before it even gets started. It was just a kiss.

Brent nodded in agreement. That was a good question. Maybe she had "relationships" so that she'd have material for her blog. Was that what Mimi was all about? Page views and comments, no matter what?

Pulling his cell phone from his pocket, Brent dialed Mimi's number. Straight to voice mail.

Later that afternoon, Mimi was a bundle of nerves as the page views on her blog grew.

"Are you insane?" MJ asked as they talked on the phone. "Why did you write about Brent?"

"No one knows that I'm talking about him."

"Please," MJ said. "He will know."

Mimi looked at her phone as it beeped and saw Brent's name scroll across the screen. She hit the deny button out of fear. Mimi sighed. "You know what, I messed up."

"Duh," MJ said. "But your comment section is blowing up."

Mimi's text alert chimed in her ear. It was Kita. Good job! Looks like you're back.

"At least the publisher is happy," Mimi said. Then another text chime. This was the message she'd been dreading. Brent's message was short and she could feel his anger through the fonts. We need to talk. Mr. Law & Order.

"Damn it, MJ, he read it."

"Are you surprised?"

"He just sent me a text."

"Then get off the phone with me, be a grown-up and talk to him. Do not respond to the text, call him."

"Nope, I don't want to adult today. I'm going for a run."

"I'm hanging up on you." Mimi could feel MJ shaking her head though the phone. When the call ended, Mimi tossed her cell phone on the desk and dropped her head. Seconds later, she picked up the phone and dialed Brent's number. Voice mail. Well, she'd done her part. Mimi headed upstairs and changed into her running gear. After three miles, she'd call him back. Then maybe she could explain why she posted about their kiss.

Brent parked his car in the lot of the complex and headed for the stairs with a head full of steam. Even though he'd missed Mimi's call, he knew they needed to talk face-to-face. As soon as he reached their floor, he saw Mimi walking out of her place dressed as if she was ready to run. Brent planted himself in front of her.

"We need to talk." The gruffness of his voice sent chills down her spine.

"Brent, I tried to call you…"

"Mimi, we're not doing this in public, though I know you like to do things that way."

She deserved that, Mimi thought as she nodded her head. Reaching into her fanny pack, she grabbed her keys and unlocked the door.

Brent was seething as he crossed the threshold. It seemed unreal to him that mere hours ago, he'd been in here making love to her. Kissing those lips, stroking that body. Brent cleared his throat and forced himself to focus on why he was standing there.

"What in the hell were you thinking?" he boomed.

"I wasn't thinking, but…"

"You know my reputation is my calling card. I've done everything above reproach my whole career. Now, with this little blog post, I look like a sleazy attorney sleeping with my clients!"

"That wasn't my intention and no one knows…"

"Stop! Just stop. If you wanted to talk about how our kiss made you feel, you knew where to find me. I'm not a damned subject for you to cover on your blog. Tell me something, did you have cameras in your bedroom last night so that you can do a video blog about what happened after the kiss?"

"Don't. I wrote that post because I was confused and angry. You'd already told me that I wasn't the kind of woman you wanted. You want the white picket fence and that's not me. But you couldn't keep your desires to yourself."

"And you couldn't open your mouth and say that to me?"

Mimi closed her eyes. Why didn't she question him, instead of giving in to her carnal needs?

"Mariah," Brent groaned. "You hide behind your blog and this persona of Mimi Collins because you're a coward."

"Excuse me?" she snapped.

"Did I stutter?"

"How dare you!"

"Really? You're going to ask me that. You put my business out there for what? Needed more page views? Didn't have another online dating site to bash? I was an easy target for you?"

"Get out," Mimi roared.

"Truth hurts, doesn't it?" Brent turned for the door and Mimi started to call his name, but it died on her lips. If he wanted to leave, then he could go. This was the reason she didn't do relationships in the first place. Men left when things didn't go their way and Brent was no different. The fact that he wouldn't listen to her explanation about why she'd written the blog and posted it made her believe that Brent wasn't any different from the other men who'd broken her heart. And she wasn't going to take that risk again.

Hours later, Brent was feeling regret for the way he'd talked to Mimi about her blog. Despite his anger, Brent knew he could've listened to Mimi. He'd allowed his father's mistakes to hold him back again. Mimi may have been wrong for sharing their intimate encounter, but he knew she wasn't trying to hurt him. But at this moment, he wondered if he'd let his past destroy his future.

Brent turned to Mimi's door and started to knock, but he dropped his hand. He had a right to be angry and she needed to know that.

But he didn't have the right to hold her responsible for his own hang-ups. Still, knowing that people could compare him to his father's ways would always make him cautious about how he lived his life. Maybe it was time for him to stop living in his father's shadow and follow his heart for once. And Mimi had taken up residency there.

Across the hall, Mimi packed an overnight bag. She had to leave. She couldn't face Brent and his anger. He knew who she was and what she did when he burst into her life and kissed her senseless.

Senseless, that's what was going on when she wrote that post. She was angry, confused and ready to do that one thing she always did when it came to affairs of the heart. Ruin it and run. She could blame it on her heartbreak, but it wasn't as if she didn't see real love. Her parents had been a perfect example. Her mother, a saint for sticking with her dad after he'd cheated on her. The pain her mother tried to hide from her, Mimi saw and vowed to never allow that to happen to her. But it had happened and she only needed one time to feel that pain. She only needed that trampling of her feelings one time to realize she was no saint like her mother. Mimi would be damned if she'd allow Brent Daniels to make her feel like the dirt on the bottom of his shoe. She wasn't going to change who she was to make him love her. Love her like she loved him.

As much as Mimi liked to believe that she was a trailblazer, living life on her own terms, if she was honest with herself, she was afraid. She was everything Brent said she was and Mimi didn't want to face it.

Her cell phone rang and she started to ignore it. But when she saw MJ's name scroll across the screen, she answered.

"Yeah?" Mimi said.

"So, did you put your big-girl panties on and talk to Brent?"

"He yelled, I listened, now I'm about to head out for a few days."

"What? Mimi, don't leave. You have to realize he has a right to be upset."

"And I don't?" She hissed, "You should've heard him, he acted as if I ruined his career."

"I'm sorry," MJ said. "So what are you going to do?"

"I'm taking a trip," she replied. "I'll call you when I get where I'm going."

"Which is where?"

"I don't know, I'm going to get in my car and drive. Maybe I'll end up in Memphis or New Orleans."

"You sound crazy."

"Whatever."

"Mimi, you don't have to run."

"I'm not running, but I won't stay here and be subjected to *him*."

"Then I guess you're going to move, since he is your neighbor?"

"Bye, MJ," Mimi said, then ended the call. She zipped her bag and grabbed her keys. As Mimi headed out to her car, she glanced over her shoulder making sure she didn't see Brent lurking around. When she didn't spot him, she hopped into her car and sped out of the parking lot. Mimi headed up Interstate 85 North, thinking that she would end up in Charlotte or Richmond for a few days. Sighing, Mimi realized that she was running and this had to stop. She pulled off on the exit for the Mall of Georgia.

Brent knocked on Mimi's door hoping to apologize for his earlier actions. He started to call her, but his cell phone rang. It was Jamal and Brent was disappointed, but he couldn't expect Mimi to call him after what happened at her place.

"What's up?" Brent asked when he answered the phone.

"I see Mimi is back. Let me guess, you're Mr. Law and Order."

"Shut up."

"I'll take that as a yes." Jamal laughed. "The comments on this post are blowing up. I think it's bigger than her Fast Love piece."

"Jamal, what do you want?" Brent gritted out. He was irritated and didn't need to hear his friend's ribbing.

"Look, I know you and how you react to things."

Brent sighed. "I messed up, man."

"So, Mr. Law and Order acted like a jackass."

"Look, this isn't the kind of publicity I need in my life," Brent said.

"You're an idiot."

"What?"

"Did you read between the lines of Mimi's post to understand what she's really saying? That woman is confused, but she has deep feelings for you."

Brent squeezed his eyes tightly. "Or she wants to get hits on her blog."

"Please tell me you didn't say that to her."

"Something like that."

"Where is she now?"

"I don't know. I just knocked on her door and no answer."

"Do you blame her? I can only imagine what you said to her and how you said it."

"So, you're skilled in reading Mimi's mind because you're sleeping with her friend?"

"Oh, wow. That's a low blow, but I understand.

That's your lack of compassion or maybe passion speaking."

"Don't worry about what I'm getting or not getting. What do you think Mimi was saying?"

"To say you're supposed to be smart, you're acting really stupid right now. The woman is into you and she isn't sure that she can live up to what you present to the world that you want. Mimi isn't the woman of your dreams, but she's probably everything you've ever needed."

Brent squeezed his eyes shut. Damn, he hated it when Jamal was right. "Now if I could only find her."

"I guess it's a good thing that MJ and I just finished talking about you clowns. Mimi is driving around aimlessly because she doesn't want to see you. My advice, which I know you've been dying to hear: get on the phone and call her."

"Then I'm hanging up on you."

Chapter 18

Mimi smiled as she listened to the representative from the New Orleans Convention and Visitors Bureau. "Your ode to New Orleans on your blog was just beautiful. I know you normally write about relationships, but there's no place like New Orleans to fall in love."

"And I'm betting that voodoo isn't a part of it at all," Mimi said.

"Not at all. I wish people had a deeper understanding of the voodoo religion and not the twisted Hollywood version," she said, her tone peppered with annoyance.

"I didn't mean to offend you," Mimi said. Though that seemed to be her thing today.

"I'm not offended, and I want to extend an invitation to you to write about the romance in the Big Easy."

"With terms and conditions, or am I able to write

what I want to write?" Mimi asked. Brent flashed in her mind. His words vibrated in her ears so loudly that she had to ask the visitors bureau lady to repeat what she'd just said.

"We want you to be you. Let your readers experience New Orleans through your eyes and hopefully come visit. Of course, we're willing to pay for your room and board while you're here."

Mimi nearly dropped her phone. This was just what she wanted, wasn't it? She wanted to get away from Atlanta and she wanted to go to New Orleans. What was stopping her?

Brent.

"Let me check my calendar and clear some things up. I could come out there in a couple of days if that works," she said.

"That sounds great. I can't wait to meet you, Mimi," she said. "Make sure you give me a call about three days before you get here so that we can send you your lodging arrangements."

"I will give you a call tomorrow," Mimi said, no longer hiding her excitement.

"Great. Thank you so much for this, Mimi."

After hanging up the phone, she headed back to Atlanta, satisfied that she wasn't running anymore. Mimi was going to build her future in New Orleans and put Brent behind her.

When she crossed into the Atlanta city limits about thirty minutes later, she didn't go home directly. She headed to her favorite restaurant on Lenox Road. Once she parked her car, she called MJ.

"Mimi," her friend said. "Where are you?"

"I'm at Houston's. It's time to celebrate. Can you meet me here?"

"On Lenox Road?"

"You know it."

"Give me about twenty minutes. I take it that you and Brent made up?"

Mimi sighed. "This has nothing to do with him. Just come on so we can eat and I can tell you the good news."

"All right," MJ said. "But I hope you had a conversation with him."

Mimi pressed End on the phone. She didn't want to think about Brent Daniels when she had New Orleans on her mind. Besides, she knew Brent wasn't looking for a woman like her. She was fine with that. At least, that was what she was trying to convince herself. In a few days, she'd be in New Orleans and Brent would be a memory.

Brent was ready to give up his vigil at Mimi's front door. Maybe she was on assignment or maybe she had a date. That thought made him shiver with jealously and anger. Who was the man she'd gone out with and did he get a chance to sample those lips? Would he have to watch that punk bring her home, walk her to the door and kiss her? What if she invited him in? Would he be able to stop himself from knocking on the door and reminding her that he'd branded her as his the nights they made love?

Brent knew he was being ridiculous. He knew that he had no right or claim to Mimi, but his imagination was driving him crazy. And he had no right to feel like this either, because he'd been ice cold to her when they'd spoken earlier. When he read the post again, he felt like the biggest asshole in America. She liked him and she was afraid—why wouldn't she be? Mimi was everything he said he didn't want. But he needed her. Pulling his cell phone from his pocket, Brent dialed Jamal again.

"Dude," Jamal said. "You're going to owe me for the rest of your life."

"What are you talking about?"

"I know where Mimi is. She and MJ are having dinner at Houston's."

Brent released a sigh of relief hearing that Mimi was with her girlfriend and not some other guy.

"Which Houston's?"

"I'm not supposed to tell you," Jamal said with a laugh. "But if I were you, I'd go get me a Biltmore sandwich from the Lenox Road one."

Brent started running for the stairs. "You're right, I owe you."

"Don't tell MJ I told you. It's too early for me to be in the doghouse."

Brent hung up on his friend as he made it to the bottom of the stairs. All Brent could think was that he hoped Mimi would hear him out and accept his apology.

"You're the luckiest woman in the world," MJ said as she and Mimi toasted her New Orleans assignment.

"I told you I wanted to move to NOLA and here it is! And the timing is just amazing," she said.

"Yes, your running plan is now in full effect," MJ said with sarcasm dripping from her lips. "At least it's tax-deductible now."

"Don't be a jerk. I wanted to travel and write, and it just so happens that someone in New Orleans recognizes my brilliance."

"Ooh," MJ said. "Your ego knows no bounds, huh?"

"Whatever. I wrote a love song to New Orleans and the right person heard it. I call that a win-win."

"If you say so. I still think you're running from your real feelings," MJ said as she sipped her champagne.

"I'm not running, I'm taking a business opportunity. I'm scouting out my future home and…"

"Running. Like stockings on a rosebush, like a tramp in church and the first lady catches her eye."

"Stop with the bad puns," Mimi said. "You're giving me a headache."

"I hope your head is ready for what's coming our way," MJ said, setting her glass aside.

Mimi turned around and locked eyes with Brent. Her smile faded like cheap paint. "What in the hell," Mimi whispered as she faced her friend. MJ shrugged.

"Evening, ladies," Brent said once he approached the table.

MJ smiled at him, while Mimi sat stone-faced with her hand on the stem of her champagne glass.

"Brent, have a seat," MJ said.

"Really," Mimi mumbled.

"Mimi, can we talk?" Brent asked.

"I've heard enough from you. What else could you possibly have to say?"

"I'm sorry."

"Excuse me," MJ said as she rose to her feet. "I have to make a call."

Mimi rolled her eyes as MJ walked away.

"Listen," Brent began, "I was wrong. My life has

been about trying to escape my father's shadow. He did some horrible things that it took me years to overcome. We have the same name. People expected me to be just like him…"

Mimi threw up her hand. "And what does this have to do with me?"

She's not going to make this easy, Brent thought as he saw the fire blazing in her eyes. "Everything and nothing," he said. "I was thinking that your blog was going to make people believe I was like him, getting involved with vulnerable women in order to win cases. I didn't want us to be tainted by that."

Mimi sipped her champagne and glared at him. Setting her glass on the table, she focused her cold stare on him. "There is no us. I'm sorry that I wrote about you on my blog and it took you to a bad place. I'm sorry that I'm not the docile woman you want to marry. I can't change who I am to be with you. I fought too hard to build my reputation and my brand."

"I understand and I'm in the same situation," he said.

"Brent," Mimi said as she turned away from him.

"Give us a chance," he said quietly.

She shook her head, then looked into his eyes. "I can't be what you want me to be. I'm leaving in a few days for New Orleans."

"What? How long are you going to be down there?"

"I'm probably going to be relocating there," Mimi said. "It's something I've been considering for a while and there's no reason for me not to explore my options."

"Sounds like you're running."

"Running from what?" she snapped.

"How you feel about us. The fact that we could have something real and not just fodder for your blog."

"I'm glad you think my life decisions revolve around you. We had sex. It was good sex, but that's all it was."

"You know it's more than that. Don't make it seem as if we…"

"I know that I'm not going to let you hurt me, Brent. I'm going to do something that you don't like again and you may decide that it's the last straw and I'm not going to sit around and wait for that to happen. It's better this way."

"Better for who?"

Mimi stood up and shook her head. "For me. Good-bye, Brent," she said, then tore out of the restaurant.

When MJ saw her friend dash out the door, she rushed over to Brent. "What in the hell just happened?"

"Mimi said she's moving to New Orleans."

"And you're going to just sit here and let it happen?"

Brent shot her a cold glare. "What am I supposed to do, grab her and force her to stay until she can admit she loves me?"

"Do you love her?" MJ asked. Brent paused. He did love Mimi. He loved her because she was nothing that he expected, nothing that he been expecting when he moved in across from her.

"I do. I love her."

"When are you going to tell her that?" MJ sighed. "I've known Mimi for a long time and as much as she tries to act like she doesn't believe in relationships and happily-ever-after, she does. Her problem is she doesn't believe it's going to happen for her. From the moment I saw you two together, I knew you were the guy who could show her that it did exist. But if you don't get off your ass and prove me right, you're going to lose her."

"I've tried to force a woman into a role she didn't want and I'm not doing it again," Brent said as he stood up. "Mimi made her decision and we're just going to have to live with it."

"You two are really a pair of idiots. Brent, Mimi has feelings for you and that scares the hell out of her. Let her know she's not in love alone," MJ said. "And before you go, you need to pay the bill. Dinner was on Mimi and you let her run out of here."

Brent shook his head and pulled some bills from his wallet and dropped them on the table. Heading for his car, he hoped what MJ said was true and he could change Mimi's mind about leaving.

Mimi clicked the buy button on the airline website. She was going to New Orleans in seven hours She'd work things out with the visitor's bureau later. Mimi had to get out of Atlanta.

Now she had to pack. Since she'd paid a mint for her last-minute ticket, she knew she had to keep her luggage to a minimum if she wanted to avoid baggage fees. She could use that money to get supplies once she settled in. She'd found a charming boardinghouse in Algiers. Mimi felt as if staying there would give her an authentic look into the city. Her first week in New Orleans, she planned to explore without the assistance of the visitors bureau. She'd talk to the locals, eat the best food and put Brent Daniels so far out of her mind that she'd have trouble realizing that he existed.

That was going to be hard, she surmised as she packed her exercise gear and underwear in a bag. Dropping down on the edge of her bed, Mimi dropped her head and stroked her forehead. She had to get out of here before Brent came back. Hearing him say he wanted a chance for them gave her pause and if she wasn't running before, she was now.

Mimi stood up and crossed over to her closet. Grabbing eight of her favorite outfits, she stuffed them in her bag, realizing that if she wanted to make a clean getaway, she would have to leave sooner rather than later.

Brent pulled into the parking lot and rushed inside to see if he could reach Mimi and tell her that he wanted her to stay and needed her in his life. Brent knew that Mimi was the second beat of his heart and watching her walk away was a pain he couldn't and wouldn't endure. He needed to find Mimi and see if they could work things out. He didn't want to lose her and he was going to do his damnedest to make sure she didn't walk out of his life. Driving home, he pulled out his cell phone and called Mimi.

Voice mail.

"I'm not playing this game with her," he thought aloud as he disconnected the call without leaving a message. Brent knew he was going to bang on her door until she answered and if push came to shove, he'd get Manny to unlock her place. Getting out of the car, Brent rushed inside, taking the stairs up to their floor two at a time. Hitting the floor, he headed for Mimi's door. He was about to knock when he saw an envelope with his name written on it. Snatching it from the door, Brent tore it open.

I know this is old-school and cliché. But I'm leaving for New Orleans tonight. It's not because of the blog post and how you felt about it, it's because I have to do what's best for me and my career. I'll never forget our time together or you. In a different time, we'd be together. We'd be everything to each other. But you and I are just two ships passing on a really big ocean. I wish you the best and a neighbor who won't need you to hang a TV in the middle of the night. Thank you for helping me with Fast Love and I promise, I won't write about you on my blog again. But if I do, LOL, it won't be under the code name Mr. Law & Order. I hope you can find some peace with your father's past and realize that everyone knows you're nothing like him. You're a good man and I know that I could've loved you. It's just that we'd end up hating each other because neither one of us is going to change.
Always,
Mariah.

Chapter 19

Mimi leaned her seat back and said a silent prayer of thanks for a half-empty plane. She didn't have to worry if someone behind her was being inconvenienced while she slept. And there were no screaming babies. She pulled out her tablet and started a draft about her journey to New Orleans.

My best friend called me a runner. In a way, she's right. I get up most mornings and run for a few miles. Right now, I'm heading over four hundred miles away from Atlanta and MJ would probably say I'm running. But this isn't running. This is me seeking adventure.

Don't get me wrong, Atlanta has been good to me. I became a grown-up in the A. The bright-eyed teenager who enrolled at Spelman College wanted to find her happy ending in the city everyone said was the Black Mecca. By now, I thought that I'd have two kids, a doting husband and a house out in Marietta. By 27, I knew this wasn't going to happen. Let's face the facts, women outnumber men in Atlanta and too many of these guys love to play the field.

I'm an only child and I don't like to share. Too many men expect us to share and buy into the whole "man shortage" crap. Yeah, not so much. Ladies, it's totally fine to be selfish. That's one of the reasons why I'm leaving for New Orleans. Because I'm being selfish. I'm not waiting for someone to choose me (shout-out to Andre 3000) because I've already chosen myself. Now, this isn't a man-hating manifesto. I'm still going to date, but I'm going to always remember the one.

I think we all get one that will set the standard for the type of person we'll date in the future. My one would've been perfect had we wanted the same things. And that means I'm not ready to change who I am for the sake of a relationship. He didn't ask me to, but I know if we were to let the breeze of love envelop us, one of us would have to change. And sadly, it's always the woman who does the changing. Hell, he might have been worth the risk, but if you've followed my blog from the beginning, you know I've been there and done that.

What came of it? He stole my credit card and bought his future wife her engagement ring. So I'm a little— okay, a lot—jaded when it comes to giving my heart away. So. I. Run.

But New Orleans is going to be an adventure. Not a rebound date—which are good things! Now, I'm not going to the Big Easy to look for a rebound romance, not as soon as the plane touches down anyway. I'm going to examine dating in another city. Is the grass greener in the Bayou? Over the next few months, I guess we will find out. Maybe my new book will be about sex in a new city.

Mimi saved the draft because she wasn't going to pay for the airplane's Wi-Fi service. Then she powered down her tablet and closed her eyes. As she drifted off to sleep, she saw Brent's face in her dreams. She opened her eyes and wondered if he'd found the note she'd left on her door. Part of her wanted to stay. When Brent sat across from her at Houston's, her heart screamed for her to take that man at his word. To listen to him and to stop being afraid.

But as usual, Mimi ignored that broken thing. How long would her relationship with Brent last when he would want to put a ring on her finger and expect her to be a typical wife? Would he expect her to change what she wrote, what she could and could not say on her blog? And what about his work? Would she be able to handle sharing her man with Atlanta? He was much like Superman—someone would always need him and she couldn't deny that it would get under her skin at some point. *Stop it*, she thought. *You're sitting here creating a fantasy in your head and there is no way that Brent wanted to marry you. He basically told you that the first time we went out. I'm not his type and I'm not changing. Why did I have to be stupid enough to fall in love with him?* Tears streamed down her cheeks. This was why Mimi Collins didn't do love. Love hurts and she was feeling too much pain.

Brent reread the little note from Mimi and shook his head. Of all the irrational things to do. She didn't even give him a chance to try to make things right. He tossed the letter on the coffee table and his cell phone rang. The unknown number spurred him to answer the phone.

"This is Brent."

"Brent?"

"Who is this?"

"Daveon."

Sighing, he knew he had to find out what his little brother wanted. "Hey, little man, what's up?'

"Well, you said I could call you if I wanted to talk. Mommy keeps crying and I don't know what to do."

"Why don't I come over and check on you guys?" Brent said. "Have you eaten dinner?"

"No. I really want some pizza."

"All right, I'm going to bring over a pizza and we'll talk, okay?"

"Okay," the little boy said, sounding relieved.

Brent pulled out of the parking lot and headed to his favorite pizza parlor. As he drove, he called Jamal to let him know what had happened with their little brother.

Part of him wanted to head to the airport and see if he could find Mimi. If only she would hear him out this time and stay in Atlanta so that they could forge a future together. But he couldn't forget the promise he'd made to his father and his brother. He said that he would be there for him, and that child sounded scared.

After getting the pizza, he headed to his brother's house. It's funny how he thought of that place now, not the place where he and Jamal did laundry in college, but as his brother's home.

Reaching for the pizza box on the passenger seat, Brent looked up at the front door and saw Daveon standing there with sorrow etched across his face. He hopped out of his car and bounded up to the steps.

"Little man, are you all right?" he asked as the boy stepped out on the porch.

Daveon wrapped his arms around his brother. "Why did he have to die?" The boy's tears seeped though Brent's shirt. He could feel his heart breaking.

Pulling back from him, Brent gripped his brother's chin and looked into his eyes. Eyes that reminded him of his and Brent Sr.'s. "God needs angels," he began. "Sometimes, those angels are people we love. When someone you loves dies and goes to heaven, that means that person is going to looking over you for the rest of your life."

"But why couldn't he stay here and look over me?"

"Well," Brent said, searching for the words. "That's why you have me."

The little boy looked at Brent with hope and questions in his eyes. "But what if you die?"

Brent's mouth dropped open. He wanted to tell him that wasn't going to die, but you couldn't say that to a heartbroken child when tomorrow was never promised. Instead he hugged his little brother tightly. "Come on, let me get the pizza and we can eat. Where's your mom?"

"Inside."

"Then let's see if she wants to get a slice of this amazing pizza." Brent gave his little brother a cheek squeeze then headed back to his car to get the pie. Once inside the house, Brent smiled when he saw pictures of Daveon and their father on the mantel above the fireplace. Brent Sr.'s smile made him forget the bad relationship they'd had at that age.

"Daveon," Donna called out. "Is someone in here?"

She walked into the living room and locked eyes with Brent. "Brent."

From the looks of her red-rimmed eyes, he could tell that she'd been crying. "I brought pizza," he said, holding up the box.

"I hope Daveon wasn't bothering you," she said.

"It's never a bother," he said, then set the pizza down on the coffee table. Daveon didn't wait for the adults to stop talking before he opened the pizza box and grabbed a huge slice.

"Brent, can we talk?" she asked as she noticed Daveon eating.

"Sure," he said as they walked into the kitchen. Sighing, she leaned against the counter and faced him.

"I know that you hated your father," she said. "I know you probably think that I'm a foolish woman for falling in love with him. But Daveon loved his father. He changed while he was locked away and…"

"Daveon is my little brother and my relationship with my father won't influence how I feel about either of you."

"Jamal was worried. He didn't know how you were going to respond to us and if you were going to be open to having a relationship with us."

"I know," he said. "I'm here for all of you. We're family now." Brent held his arms out to her and gave her a tight hug.

"Thank you," she said as she sobbed quietly.

"Let's see if Daveon left us any pizza," he said as they released each other and headed back into the living room. For the rest of the evening, the new family ate pizza and watched a superhero movie.

Brent tucked Daveon into bed and kissed his brother on the forehead. From the doorway, Donna beamed.

"You are so good with him," she said as Brent crossed over to him. "Your dad would be proud."

Brent smiled to keep from saying something negative about his father. "Donna, any time you guys need me, call me."

"Thank you, Brent."

Heading to his car, Brent pulled out his cell phone and called Jamal. Part of him felt like a jerk for calling his friend to fish out MJ's phone number when he hadn't even talked to him about what happened at his mother's house.

"Man, you're going to live a long time," Jamal said. "Mom and I were just talking about you. You did a really good thing tonight."

"I made a promise to our little brother and I'm going to keep it," Brent said.

"That's good to know. He's really scared and my mama is taking things really hard right now."

"I noticed. But between the two of us, we'll help them through this."

"How did things go with Mimi?"

Brent sighed. "She's gone."

"Gone?"

"Left me a note that she was going to New Orleans. I was hoping you could give me MJ's number so that I could find out where she is."

"Hold on," Jamal said. Brent could hear him whispering and then MJ came to the phone.

"Brent, did you say Mimi went to New Orleans? I thought she wasn't leaving for a couple of days. My God, she is really out of her mind."

"Where is she staying in New Orleans?"

"I don't know. We had only talked about the commission she'd gotten from the visitors bureau. I didn't even get the full details about it. Let me call her."

"You know what," Brent said. "Don't worry about it. She made her decision and there's no need to try to force her into doing something she doesn't want to do. If she wants to start over with her life down there, then what right do I have to try to change her mind?"

"Because you love her, silly," MJ said with a sigh. "Y'all are two exasperating people."

"She left a note. I'm just going to take her at her written word," Brent said. "If this is what's in Mimi's heart, I shouldn't stop her from following it."

"Fine, enjoy being miserable." She disconnected the call and Brent looked down at his phone. Then he brushed off any second thoughts. Mimi made her decision, and he wasn't going to act like some lovesick puppy and follow her to Louisiana.

One Month Later

Brent snapped his briefcase shut after presenting his motions in his third case of the morning. He was two for three so far and the judge had just granted a continuance in this case. Glancing down at his watch, he decided that he should go and get some real food before his one o'clock meeting with Willis Arrington, former director of a nonprofit in the city. Willis was suing the nonprofit because he was fired after questioning disappearing donations.

His phone buzzed, indicating that he had a text. Pulling his phone out, he read what Jamal had to say.

Have you read Mimi's blog lately?

Brent ignored the message. He tried to pretend that he hadn't been thinking about Mimi or the fact that he hadn't heard from her since she left a month ago. And he wasn't going to admit that he read her blog every day trying to figure out if there was a new man in her life.

And he wasn't going to tell Jamal that he was having dinner with Denisha tonight. When she'd called him last week, he wondered if he'd been too hasty in ending the relationship. She claimed that she'd changed.

He'd changed as well. Maybe they needed this second chance. Or maybe he was just trying to replace memories of Mimi.

Mimi walked into the bookstore along Frenchmen Street feeling nervous and excited at the same time. She'd had several book signings in Atlanta and around the metro area. But that was home. Her book was about Atlanta. This was New Orleans. What if readers in New Orleans didn't care for her books or her blog?

"Are you going in or are you just going to stand in the doorway like a dunce?" MJ asked.

"And here I thought you were supposed to be moral support."

"Girl, please, I'm here for the beignets." MJ laughed and patted Mimi on the shoulder. "Don't be nervous. This is what you wanted, remember?"

What she wanted was Brent. Mimi could admit it now. After thirty days away from him and hearing more lame pickup lines than the law should allow, Mimi knew that she'd messed up big-time. Sure, there could've been a nice guy in the bunch that she'd met while traversing the city and getting acclimated to the nightlife. Of course, she had to go out and find things to write about. She'd been aching for adventure; now she just ached for Brent.

"How's Jamal?" Mimi asked as she walked forward.

"I'm not going to fall down this briar patch, sis. You could care less how Jamal is doing."

"If I didn't care I wouldn't have asked."

"Well, Brent seems to be doing well. He's working a lot and spending a lot of time with his little brother. He stopped asking about you a week ago. I can't believe you left him a Dear John letter."

"I didn't ask about Brent."

"But you were going to. Mimi, you know you're crazy, right? That man loves you and you love him."

The owner of the bookstore, Kim Knight, spotted Mimi and waved at her. "Welcome!" she said as she crossed over to her and enveloped her in a hug. "I'm so excited to have you here. We're expecting a huge turnout. Half of your books have already been sold."

"That sounds great! Kim, this is my best friend Michael Jane."

"Michael?"

"It's a long story. Everyone calls me MJ," she said as she shook hands with the comely bookseller. "Your store is amazing. Thanks for hosting Mimi."

"I have been addicted to her blog for years!" Kim said, then turned to Mimi. "I have to ask, what happened to Mr. Law and Order?"

MJ started coughing to cover her laughter as Mimi stood there with her mouth wide open.

"Umm, I guess you'll have to keep following to find out," she stammered. Kim led Mimi and MJ to the area where the reading and signing would take place. Mimi was excited to see a plate of beignets and a carafe of coffee.

"If you need anything, just let me know," Kim said.

"Everything looks amazing. Thank you so much," Mimi said. But just like Kim, she was wondering what happened to Mr. Law and Order.

Brent was late for dinner and when he approached the table where Denisha sat, she looked as if she'd eaten a whole lemon.

"Sorry I'm late," he said, and leaned in to kiss her cheek. She turned her head away from him.

"The more things change, the more *you* stay the same," she hissed.

"Had a bad day?"

"No, this is just reminding me of our relationship. Late for dinners, late for shows. Just late all the time."

"And I thought you'd given up nagging," Brent said as he took a seat across from her.

Denisha sighed. "I'm sorry, but when we spoke on the phone and you were talking about how much things have changed and how you changed, I thought we were going to have a second chance at the magic we could've had."

Brent smirked and leaned back in his chair. "The magic. Denisha, despite all the letters behind your name, all the organizations that you belong to, you're still the same social-climbing wannabe that I left behind."

"Did you invite me here to insult me?"

"No, I thought there was something that I'd missed

out on with you, with us. This was a mistake. I wasn't thinking clearly when I agreed to this."

"Oh, really? You're rude. And I guess I was supposed to be so excited to have dinner with you that I was going to forget that I have needs and deserve more than what you offered me. I see you sold the house."

"Yes."

"Why? It was in a great neighborhood. I hoped that we'd raise our kids there…"

"And film that reality show, too?"

Denisha fiddled with the napkin on the edge of the table. "You just can't let that go?"

"I've never been one to seek the spotlight. But I see that you've been making a lot of good things happen these days. Especially at the Atlanta University Center."

Denisha smiled. "You've noticed."

"Yes, I have."

"And so have some of Bravo's TV producers," she said, her eyes glittering with excitement. "I was hoping we could do a few episodes together."

Brent shook his head and laughed—not at her but himself. "That's one thing that hasn't changed, Denisha. I'm not parading around on TV to prove that I'm a mover and shaker in Atlanta. My work speaks for itself."

She shook her head. "Still on your high horse. Or are you still trying not to be confused with your father?"

Brent rose to his feet. "Goodbye, Denisha."

"Brent, wait!"

He strode out of the restaurant and didn't look back. Meeting with Denisha proved one thing: he needed to be with Mimi. Brent hopped in the car and pulled out his cell phone. He logged on to the Delta Air Lines website and booked a flight to New Orleans. He was going to get the woman he loved back into his life.

Chapter 20

Mimi took a bow as the capacity crowd clapped for her after she read a passage from her manuscript.

"I can't wait to read it," one woman cried out.

"Make sure you buy copies for your friends," Mimi said with a grin. "Before we go, I'm going to open the floor up to questions."

The hands shot up. Mimi pointed to a woman wearing a purple Got Books shirt. "Yes?"

"I loved your book, Mimi, and I read your blog all the time. But I have to know, did you and Mr. Law and Order work things out?"

Mimi grabbed her cup of water and took a big sip. "Well, I'm here and I'm alone, so what do you think?" She laughed nervously.

A few of the women in the crowd mumbled "aww," then one called out, "You know you messed that up."

"Any more questions, not about Mr. Law and Order?" she asked, then glanced at MJ, who was hiding her grin behind a cup of coffee.

When things started to wrap up at the store, Mimi knew she needed a few adult drinks. "Mimi," MJ said. "Are you going to call Mr. Law and Order?"

"Shut up. And for the record, if Brent wanted to talk to me, he would've called me. My number hasn't changed. You were able to get in touch with me. I've taken the hint. He's probably with his ideal woman right how."

MJ shook her head. "I'm going to tell you the same thing I told him when he got your Dear John note—enjoy being miserable."

"How about we go and enjoy some hurricanes?" Mimi said, then rolled her eyes.

"That sounds like a great plan. I hear they are delicious."

Mimi smiled. "I know the perfect place." The two women headed down Frenchmen Street to hang out at one of Mimi's favorite watering holes.

Brent dialed Mimi's number and hoped that she would answer. "Hello?" she said, though it was hard to hear her with the background noise.

"Mimi, it's me."

"Brent?"

"You remember," he said with a chuckle.

"Hold on for a second, I'm going to step outside so that I can hear you."

It felt as if an hour passed before Mimi came back to the phone. "Brent, how have you been?"

"You want the truth or some PC answer?" he asked.

"Always the truth," she said with a laugh.

"I miss you, Mimi."

"It took you a month to realize that?"

"So if we're following that logic, then I guess the feeling wasn't mutual."

He heard her sigh, then giggle. "I miss you, too."

"What are you doing tomorrow, then?"

"Taking a tour of a haunted plantation."

"That does sound very adventurous. After hearing ghost stories, I'm sure you're not going to want to sleep alone."

"And I'm supposed to wait for you to drive down and keep me safe from the things that go bump in the night?"

"No. I'm going to fly."

"Really?"

"Yes," he said. "My flight leaves tomorrow after court."

"Are you serious?"

"Very. We need to have a face-to-face conversation and my mouth is watering to taste you."

"Brent," she whispered.

"Mimi, this last month has been hell. And I'm not going through another thirty days like this. Hell, not another day."

"Has anything changed?" she asked.

"We'll talk about it when I get there. Can you pick me up from the airport or do I need to rent a car?"

"I can make arrangements to come get you," she said. "What time does your plane land?"

"Six thirty, your time," he said.

"Then I guess I will see you tomorrow," she said,

and he could've sworn she sounded happy. Brent couldn't wait to board the plane.

Mimi returned to the bar with a huge smile on her face. MJ, who had been approached by two handsome Creole men with drinks in their hands, nearly leaped from her stool. "What took you so long?"

"That was Brent."

"Really?"

Mimi nodded and grabbed her friend's hand. "He's coming here tomorrow."

"Well, looks like you two have finally come to your senses. So what's going to happen now?"

"First, I need to rent a car," she said, then glanced at the two men at the bar. "Then we have to get rid of them."

"Oh, that's easy. Come on," MJ said as she walked in the direction of the bar. "Hey guys."

"Hello, beautiful ladies," the taller man said. "I didn't think you were going to come back."

"Well, my girlfriend and I made up. Sorry, I used you to make her jealous," MJ said with a smile as she wrapped her arm around Mimi's shoulder.

Mimi played along, leaning her head against MJ's shoulder. "We're going to go now. Thank you for the drinks," Mimi said with a wink. As they walked out of the bar, Mimi couldn't help but laugh at the shocked looks on those men's faces.

"All right," MJ said once they made it to the sidewalk. "So that you don't have to go looking for a rental, how about you book me a flight back to Atlanta and keep my car?"

"Really?"

MJ nodded. "I'm sure Jamal will come get me when I land."

Mimi leaned back and looked at her friend. "What's the real deal with you two?"

"We're good friends. I'm not setting myself up to get hurt again," she said. "I know where Jamal stands and he knows where I stand."

"And where is that?"

"Don't worry about me. I got this. You and Brent need to get your stuff together. Lord knows that man has been miserable without you. And as much as you claim you wanted to be in New Orleans, I don't see you bursting with happiness and joy."

"Oh, shut up. I just hope he doesn't think I've changed. Did I miss him? Yes. But I'm still me and I'm not turning myself inside out because I'm in love."

"If it's real, you two will find a way to make it work. And from what I've seen, this isn't a one-sided thing like me and Nic."

"Have you heard from him lately?"

"Well, he's still my client, so I hear from him through my representative. He claims that he's going to move his business if I don't get back to working on his account."

"Emotional blackmail," Mimi murmured.

"I really don't need his business. But I think it's very interesting how he's needing to hear from me now." MJ rolled her eyes. "I'm guessing it has something to do with seeing Jamal and me out at Watershed on Peachtree."

"I thought you didn't like that place?"

"They have a new chef and it's delicious now. Jamal

likes peach cobbler and kissing after taking a huge bite," she said with her eyes glimmering.

"TMI! Let me guess, that's what Nic walked in on?"

She nodded. "But that's not important. You need to get my ticket and get me to the airport so that you can pick Brent up tomorrow. He makes you happy and you deserve happiness for a change."

Mimi closed her eyes and imagined Brent walking down the corridor and into her arms. Would he have a beard now? Did he let his hair grow out? Had he lost weight? Gained more muscle?

"Oh snap," Mimi said. "We have to go, I need to find something to wear!"

MJ shook her head as she and Mimi took off down the sidewalk.

Jamal yawned as he pulled up to Brent's place. He wasn't surprised to see his best friend standing in the parking lot like a kid excited about the first day of school. Lowering the window on the passenger side, he called out, "Anxious much?"

"Shut up. You know I don't like being late," Brent said as he strode over to the car and opened the back door to toss his bag in.

"I thought you had a later flight?"

"Got an upgrade, and I've waited too long to see Mimi as it is."

"Glad you two came to your senses. Now MJ can stop hand-holding her and get back here." The smile on Jamal's face was telling and shocking to Brent. He'd never seen his friend talk about a woman this way.

"So, this thing with MJ, it's serious?"

"We're taking it one day at a time and it's been some

really good days," he replied. "But it is too early to talk about this, especially when I haven't had any coffee."

Brent slid in the passenger seat. "Hell has officially frozen over," he said with a laugh.

"You want to walk to Hartsfield-Jackson?" Jamal quipped. "You worry about yourself and Mimi. Let me and MJ do us."

Brent threw up his hands. "Just do me a favor. Don't mess things up with MJ. The moment you two come into the bedroom with me and Mimi, I'm going to break your jaw."

Jamal sucked his teeth. "I can say the same thing to you. But, oops, you and Mimi have already joined us in bed because of this little standoff. What made you come to your senses?"

"Denisha."

"Aww, hell. What in the…"

"When Mimi left, I was pissed. So I made a bad decision and had dinner with Denisha. She looked better on paper than she did sitting across the table from me. Same stuff, different day. I knew then that I won't be happy without Mimi."

"I'm still waiting to hear one thing," Jamal said.

"What?"

"*Jamal, you were right.*"

"Keep waiting," Brent quipped.

Mimi woke up about 5:00 a.m. feeling as if it were Christmas morning. She glanced over at MJ, who was knocked out. Mimi reached for her tablet and did something she'd promised herself she would do again— write about Brent. But this time she'd be smart about it and make it a story of two "other" people.

Love is a fickle thing. Unexplainable and weird. That's why so many of us are confused, upset and just plain through with love. That's where girl was when she met guy. She was done with the games, with the need to impress, and wanted nothing more than to date and move on. She wasn't into Netflix and chill, nor was she into commitment. Sounds weird to say a woman doesn't want a commitment since the line on the sisters—especially the ones in the South—is that we're all trying to get married after the second date.

Guy, on the other hand, knew what he wanted and from what he said, it wasn't her. He wanted the relationship, the big house out in the suburbs and kids. Commitment should've been his middle name. But guy had his own rules about how things should go in the confines of being with him. He's not a man who likes to be around mistakes, and girl made a big one. Well, two if you count the fact that she fell in love with him and tried to pretend that it didn't matter. Tried to pretend that moving about five hundred miles away from him would change her feelings, make her think of something else, like her career.

Girl was offered dates and girl turned them down—even from the guy who looked like Lenny Kravitz. Girl really thinks it may have been Lenny, but she was so engulfed in thoughts of guy that she couldn't see the forest for the trees. She'd been wondering if he'd thought about her, if he'd turned down dates, or was he living the life? Seriously, she hadn't heard from him in almost a month and as the old saying goes, Out of sight, out of mind.

And just when girl was ready to toss away her feelings and wrap her broken heart in Bubble Wrap, she got a call from guy saying the same thing she felt. And it didn't feel like she'd won; it didn't feel like she had control. It felt good. And that's how a girl and guy should fall in love.

Mimi published her post and smiled. She just hoped the real thing lived up to what she wrote. Glancing at the clock, she silently started the countdown until she'd see Brent.

"Flight 3209 to New Orleans has been delayed," the voice over the public address system droned. "We apologize for the delay. Once the fog lifts, we will begin boarding. Thank you for your patience."

Patient was the one word that didn't describe Brent at this moment. He stalked the waiting area outside the gate like a man possessed. He wanted to be on the plane on his way to his woman. His woman. A woman he almost let go for all the wrong reasons.

Mimi had been worried about being his ideal woman, when Brent was the one who needed to wonder if he was ideal for her. He didn't want to change her—he loved every part of Mimi. Every outspoken and quirky bit of her. Now it was time to prove it. As soon as this damn fog lifted.

Pulling out his phone, he sent her a text telling her he'd planned to surprise her and arrive in New Orleans early, but Mother Nature had other ideas.

Chapter 21

Mimi smiled at the text she received from Brent. He was just as anxious as she was and she loved it.

"MJ," she called out. "Are you ready?"

"Seriously? You're rushing me?"

"Yes," Mimi replied. "Brent's coming in on an earlier flight and there's a bit of a weather issue in Atlanta."

MJ walked out of the bathroom dressed in a pink-and-yellow romper. "So you want to drop me off at the airport and have me sit there like I'm Tom Hanks?"

"No, I want you to go on the tour with me, then I'm going to drop you off at the airport."

"That haunted tour? Not on your life!"

"Come on, it'll be fun," Mimi said.

"There is a reason why I don't watch horror movies and that's because being scared is not fun."

"Then think of it as a history lesson. Come on, when will you ever have this chance again?"

"Fine, but if I end up having nightmares, I will be calling you in the middle of the night no matter what you're doing or who you're with." MJ stroked her chin. "Are you coming back to Atlanta?"

Mimi paused. In all of the excitement about her pending reunion with Brent, she hadn't thought about what this meant for her assignment in New Orleans or her future. She wanted to be here. Wanted a change, and she thought this was it. How could she give up what she wanted because she loved him? Was he willing to give up anything for her?

"I don't know," she said. "Let's go." Mimi slipped into her walking shoes, but her mind was no longer on the tour but on what her future was going to look like now.

Two hours later, Brent was seated in first class listening to a podcast of places to visit while in New Orleans. It had been a long time since he'd visited Louisiana and he couldn't help but remember the last time he'd been there. Hounded by reporters after his parentage had been discovered following his graduation from law school. It wasn't one of his favorite places, but he'd pretend it was as long as Mimi was there. He couldn't help but wonder how much she wanted to be there. Had the trip to New Orleans been her escape plan or something that had been in the works for a while?

"Sir," a flight attendant asked. "May I get you a drink?"

Brent shook his head and leaned his seat back; his

attention was no longer on the podcast, but on Mimi and how they were going to make this work.

Mimi glanced at her watch as she and MJ followed their tour guide around the Laura Plantation. Had Brent left Atlanta yet? "And," the tour guide said, causing Mimi to snap to attention, "though these are the slave quarters, something magical happened here about three years ago."

"What was that?" Mimi asked, thinking of how horrible conditions had to be for the slaves who had to call these small cabins home. What kind of magic could've happened here?

"Two visitors were on the tour. And the woman stood right here and started trembling. There was a man here from Baton Rouge and he wrapped his arms around her. As it turned out, they were descendants of a group of slaves who were brought here and led a great escape as the plantation changed hands again. Those two visitors here that day were married about a year later. As it turns out, her great-great-great-grandmother and his great-great-great-grandfather were the leaders of the escape."

"Wow," Mimi and MJ said in concert.

"For some people, it's all about ghosts and being scared when you hear *haunted tour.* But it's more than that."

Mimi nodded. "That's a wonderful story. Any idea how to get in contact with them?"

The tour guide nodded. "I sure do. Are you going to write about them on your blog?"

"Of course," Mimi replied with a smile.

"You're getting sappy," MJ whispered to her friend.

"I could always write about you and Jamal to bring my edge back."

"I'll sue you, and I'm not going to back down like Fast Love," she gritted out.

"Yeah, right," Mimi said. The tour guide glanced at them, but kept silent.

"Can we get a few pictures?" Mimi asked. "I can't wait to write about this on my blog."

"That's awesome, and while you're getting your pictures, I'll get the couple's contact information for you," the tour guide replied excitedly.

"Thanks," Mimi said as she pulled out her smartphone and began snapping pictures of the plantation. When her phone chimed, indicating that she had a text, Mimi nearly forgot about the pictures.

I'm about to land.

"We have to wrap this up," Mimi told MJ. "Brent's about to land."

"Good thing I'm packed," she said with a smile. "I'm going to text Jamal and let him know what time to pick me up."

"Do you think I'm expecting too much?" Mimi asked.

"What are you expecting?"

She sighed and watched the tour guide heading in her direction. "Magic."

Brent wanted to kiss the ground as he walked off the plane. But he kept his composure. Mimi would be there soon enough, and since he only had a carry-on bag, he could bypass the baggage claim at the Louis

Armstrong airport. Glancing at his watch, he hoped that he hadn't caused too much of an uproar in her day. But honestly, he really didn't care. His desire to see her trumped his need for fair play. The moment he stepped out to the corner where the travelers waited for taxis and their family, he spotted her. Dressed in a yellow sundress and red pumps, Mimi was a vision. His body hummed with want and desire.

"Brent!" she exclaimed as she crossed over to him. He closed the space between them, pulling her into his arms and kissing her deep and slow.

Neither of them cared about the stares passersby gave them as their kiss deepened and his hands roamed her back. Mimi pressed her hand against his chest. "Whoa," she breathed as their lips parted. "I missed you, too."

"Mimi, I'm sorry and I missed you more than you'll ever know."

She poked him in the side. "Then why did it take you a month to call?"

Brent tilted his head to the side. "'Cause every time I started to pick up the phone I read your note again."

She dropped her head. "I was running. I should've stayed and explained what I'd written and…"

"Next time, give me a better code name."

She smiled broadly. "Let's get out of here," she said as they headed to the car hand in hand. Once they were in the car, Mimi turned to Brent. "Are you hungry?"

He gave her a slow-once over. "Starving. Where are you staying? Some swanky spot in the French Quarter?"

"Actually, I'm staying in Algiers Point. It's about

twelve miles from here, but we can stop in the Quarter if you'd like."

"We don't have to do that," he said as she pulled out of the underpass. "I'm pretty sure what I want isn't in the Quarter."

A heated blush turned her cheeks red. "Is that so?"

"Yes."

They drove along in a charged silence until Brent spotted a secluded road to the left. "Pull over there," he said.

"Why, what's wrong?" she asked as she turned down the road.

Brent reached over and placed the car in Park. "I told you, I am starving," he said, then lifted her dress. Mimi shivered as she felt the heat of his breath against her panties.

"I've been thinking about this for a long time," he said as he pulled the crotch of her lace panties to the side. He licked her wetness as if she were melting ice cream. "Brent," she cried out as he lashed her throbbing bud. "Brent."

"You taste so good. Missed your sweetness," he said before wrapping his lips around her wet ones. Mimi squirmed and moaned as his tongue darted in and out of her. Her slit was wet with desire and her thighs trembled with anticipation. Lick. Suck. Lick.

"Brent!"

Suck. Lick. Suck.

"OhmigodBrent, I can't take it."

"Come for me. Let me taste you."

Shivering, Mimi exploded as his tongue brushed against her sensitive pearl one more time. His face was shiny with her release. "I-I, whoo!" she exclaimed as her heart rate slowed to a normal pace. "That was… I'm not sure if I can drive right now."

He stroked her inner thigh with his fingertips. "Maybe you don't need to drive right now. I think I need to taste you again and twelve miles is a long way away."

"Brent, you're so bad."

"But you feel so good. You can't blame me."

She shook her head. "But we can't go to jail in Orleans Parish, either. Can you imagine the scandal?" Mimi laughed.

"You do have a point because what I want to do to you right now is very scandalous." He slipped his hands underneath her dress and pulled her panties down.

"What are you…"

"Step out of them. I just need a reminder of what I have to wait twelve miles for," he said.

Mimi shook her head, but followed his directions. "Who are you and what have you done with Brent Daniels?" she asked as she tossed her panties at him. He tucked the lacy undies into his pocket.

"I'm right here, ready to claim what's mine."

"You think it's going to be that easy?" Mimi teased.

Brent leaned back in the seat and smiled. "I know it is."

The drive to Mimi's place seemed to be electric. Her body was tense and ready to be claimed, even if she tried to pretend she wasn't going to make it easy for him. Pulling up to the pink boardinghouse, Brent smiled. "I can see you staying here," he said. "Did you bring the PlayStation?"

Mimi laughed. "No. Who would've hung the TV? You were in Atlanta, in your feelings," she said.

"That's not funny because it's true. I mean, what was that Dear John note supposed to do, make me happy?"

She faced him, the playfulness gone from her face. "Brent, can we be honest for a minute?" she began. "I left because you and I don't see eye to eye on how this is supposed to work."

"This is how it works," Brent said. "I love you. I love everything about you. There's nothing about you I want to change."

"But you want a traditional life and I'm not about that life."

He stroked her cheek, then pulled her face close to his. "You seem to think you have me all figured out," Brent said, then brushed his lips across hers. "I've had some time to think about this whole picture-perfect life and maybe it isn't everything I thought it would be. Let me be clear on one thing: without you none of this matters. I didn't come to New Orleans to change anything about you."

Mimi wanted to melt in his arms. "Brent, I don't…"

He put his finger to her lips. "Mimi, I want a future with you in it."

"What if my future is here in New Orleans?"

"There are these things called planes, trains and automobiles. Ever heard of them?"

"Smart-ass," she quipped.

"What do you want, Mimi? You want to keep hiding behind your computer or do you want to have a real life with a man who loves you?"

Her mouth formed the shape of an *O*. She wanted to say yes. Brent made it sound so simple, so easy. But…

"What is it, Mimi?"

"I'm scared," she said. "I've never felt this way before and you struck a chord when you said I hide behind my blog. But it's become a part of who I am. If you think I'm going to give that up…"

"I don't," he said, then kissed her on the tip of her nose. "The only thing I need you to give up is…" Brent pulled her panties out of his pocket and twirled them around his index finger. "Let's take this inside."

Mimi nodded and opened her car door. Brent followed suit and they dashed inside. Trembling, she unlocked the door. They walked into the spacious room Mimi had called home for the past month. Brent didn't take a moment to absorb the interior, the sea-foam-green walls and yellow curtains, didn't care about the aqua-blue bedspread with the pale pink roses. As soon as she closed the door, Brent pressed her against the wooden door. He brought his mouth down on top of hers as he lifted her leg and wrapped it around his waist. Their tongues danced a tango as his fingers toyed with her throbbing clit.

Mimi's soft moans filled the air as Brent lifted her up and carried her a few feet to the bed.

"Brent," she whispered as she watched him strip out of his clothes. His naked body was a sight for sore eyes and hungry lips. She released a slow breath as he lowered himself on the bed.

"Mimi," he said as he eased the strap of her dress down. "You're so beautiful." Their lips met and Brent devoured her mouth as if it were the sweetest fruit he'd ever tasted.

She moaned as his tongue traced her lips. With one hand, he exposed her breast and kissed her satin skin. Brent's tongue flicked across her pebble-hard nipple.

With his free hand, Brent massaged her other breast while continuing to nibble on her nipple. Mimi arched her body into him, giving Brent carte blanche to control her and give her the pleasure she desired.

Pleasing her was his mission as he dropped his hand from her breast and slipped it between her thighs. His nimble fingers darted in and out of her wetness.

"Yes," she cried, tossing her head back in bliss. Brent peeled her dress from her body as he eased down to her hips. Brent spread her legs and planted his face between them. She was wet, hot and delicious. Brent licked and sucked her until Mimi grew hoarse from screaming his name.

Brent pulled back from her, taking joy in watching the sated look on her face. She ran her hand down the center of his chest as she caught her breath. "Umm," she moaned. "Need you." Mimi reached down and stroked his erection. "Need this."

"It's all yours." Brent drove deep inside her. Mimi wrapped her legs around his waist, pulling him in further. She ground against him slowly. Brent matched her rhythm. Rocking at a pace that made every sensation and tingle feel like an ocean wave hitting them in the face on a cold day. Explosive.

"Mimi, Mimi," he groaned as he reached his climax. Wrapped in each other's arms, they drifted off to sleep—satisfied and sated.

Mimi woke up with a start, almost believing that the past few hours had been an amazing Technicolor dream. Sure, she was in bed naked, but she was also alone. It wasn't until she heard the faint sound of the shower that it sank in. Brent was here. Brent had proclaimed his love for her. He'd said all of those amazing things about wanting to be with her. But what did she really want? Was she truly ready for this?

"Glad to see you're awake," Brent said as he walked into the room with a towel wrapped around his waist.

"It's even better to know that I wasn't dreaming," she said as she inched toward the edge of the bed. "Good shower?"

He shrugged. "Could've been better. You should've been there."

Mimi laughed and yawned. "Next time."

Brent sat on the bed beside her and stroked her wild hair. "Mimi," he said with a smile, "you're the most beautiful woman I've ever met. Inside and out. I love you more than I thought I'd love someone."

"So, how do we do this?" she asked. "I never knew real love until now. Honestly, I'm scared."

"Don't be."

"I have a few more days here with my assignment and then I was going to look for some property."

"You want to move to New Orleans?"

She shrugged. "I thought I did. Then again, I have a mobile career and I just need a base of operations."

"Louisiana isn't a bad place," he said. "I mean, if that's where you want to be. We can get a nice place in the Quarter if you like."

"We?"

"Yes, we're in this together. Whether it's Atlanta or New Orleans, we're going to make our life together." Brent kissed her lips gently. "You just have to answer one question for me."

"What's that?" she asked.

"Will you marry me?"

Tears sprang into Mimi's eyes. "Are you serious?"

He held her face between his hands and brushed his nose against hers. "Very. Marry me, Mimi."

"Yes, I will." Brent kissed her and wiped her tears at the same time.

"I love you, Mimi."

"I love you, too," she replied.

Epilogue

"Mimi Collins is getting married," MJ said as she pinned her friend's veil on her head. "I still don't believe it."

Mimi glanced at her reflection in the mirror. "Amazing, isn't it?"

"I think I just walked into the twilight zone," MJ said as Mimi stood up. "You ranted against marriage for years. You didn't want to be Mrs. Anybody. Remember that?"

"I also remember you saying Nic was the man for you and look at you and Jamal."

MJ blushed and turned away from her friend. "I'm just taking it one day at a time," she said. "No rushing into my feelings this time."

Mimi rose to her feet and smiled at her reflection. Three months ago, she wouldn't have believed that she'd be standing here in a wedding dress. The ivory dress hit her right above her knees and the heart-shaped neckline gave just enough cleavage to be sexy and classy. Her mother's diamond pendant hung right above her breasts and she knew Brent would love it.

Last night had been the first night in three months that they'd spent apart. But he still had his traditions, and spending the night with his wife-to-be before the wedding was one thing he wasn't giving up.

He hadn't even responded to her sexy text messages until this morning. You better live up to all of this. I have it in writing.

Mimi took a deep breath. "I'm getting married."

Brent tugged at his bow tie. In less than thirty minutes, he was going to be married to the woman of his dreams. A woman he couldn't wait to call Mrs. Daniels. Glancing to his left, he saw his mother watching him with pride gleaming in her eyes. She'd met Mimi last month and immediately fell in love with her.

"She is going to keep you straight," his mother had said after dinner.

"What do you mean?"

"Oh, Miss Mimi is something else. She says what she thinks and she isn't that impressed by you, son. I like her a lot."

"Good," he had said as he refilled her glass of wine. "We're getting married."

"Thank God! I'm glad you're marrying a real woman and not those vapid women who have no more to offer than their bodies and the promise of getting pregnant. Don't get me wrong, I want a couple of grandkids. Y'all are going to make cute babies."

"No pressure, right?" Brent laughed as his mother took a sip of her wine. Mimi had returned to the dining room with cheesecake and when his mother rose to her feet and gave her a tight hug, Brent knew he'd made the best decision of his life.

"You breathing?" Jamal asked, breaking into Brent's thoughts.

"I'm good, just ready to say 'I do' and get on with the honeymoon."

Jamal shook his head. "Man down," he said as he buttoned his jacket.

"You're next. I've seen you and MJ together and you know what they say when best friends get married."

"MJ isn't like that. Her mind is on her money," Jamal said, and Brent could've sworn his friend looked a little upset about it. "Anyway, Daveon is excited you're letting him be a part of your big day."

"Where is he?" Brent asked.

"Last time I saw him, he was trying to sneak some cake squares from the baker."

Brent smiled. "That's my little brother."

"Mom's going to try to keep his suit clean. I have to say, I'm surprised this isn't more traditional. I expected your wedding to be one of those affairs in a castle and whatnot. But here we are in a historic plantation in New Orleans. You said Mimi took a tour of this place and had to get married here, huh?"

Brent nodded. Instead of wedding gifts, their guests made donations to preserve the historic landmark. The idea of giving back made Brent love Mimi even more.

"This was Mimi's idea and it was a good one. That's why I agreed to putting pictures from the wedding on her blog."

Jamal clasped his hands together. "Then let's get y'all hitched. I'm glad you both came to your senses."

"Let's go. I'm ready to kiss my future."

Brent and Jamal headed into the foyer, which had been converted into a pink and white altar. It had been his mother's idea. Brent would've jumped through a neon-green circus hoop and stood in the middle of a boxing ring to say "I do" to Mimi.

Turning toward the door, Brent waited for his woman to walk in. And if he was expecting to hear "The Wedding March," he was mistaken. The sounds of Prince singing "Adore," made him look at the door. MJ walked in with a big grin on her face. Brent cast a glance at Jamal, who seemed mesmerized by her body-hugging silver gown. Their eyes met and Brent didn't miss the undercurrent of desire that bubbled between them. That was quickly pushed out of his mind when he saw Mimi in the doorway. *Beautiful* was an under-statement. Stunning. Amazing. Breathtaking.

"Mimi," he whispered as she approached him. He drew her into his arms as he drank in her image. He should've known not to expect a princess dress or a gown featured in a bridal magazine.

"Slow down," Jamal quipped. "You have to get married first."

"Shut up," Mimi gritted out before kissing Brent.

"Well," the justice of the peace said as she cleared her throat. "We haven't gotten to that part yet."

The group gathered in the room laughed. "I'm going to have to make this quick," the justice said. "Dearly beloved, these two are here to get married. They love each other and love the community. Now, Mimi, do you promise to love, honor and cherish Brent Daniels for the rest of your life?"

"I do," she replied as she stared into his sparkling eyes.

"And," the justice said, "do you promise to give him a better name on your blog when you write about him?"

More laughter. "Or maybe don't write about me at all," Brent said, leaning in and kissing her cheek.

"Don't give me a reason," Mimi replied with a wink.

"All right," the justice said. "Brent, do you promise to love, honor and cherish Mariah Collins for the rest of your life and don't give her a reason to write about you on her blog?"

"I do," Brent said with a huge smile.

"By the power vested in me by the state of Louisiana, I now pronounce you husband and wife. You may…"

Brent didn't wait for clearance; he pulled Mimi into his arms and kissed her: slow, deep, like he could do this forever.

"Umm," Mimi moaned as their lips parted. "I definitely have a new name for you on the blog."

"And what's that?" he asked as he pulled her closer.

"The love of my life."

* * * * *

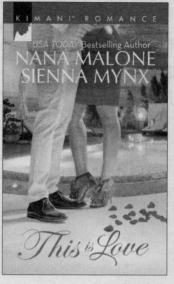

REQUEST YOUR FREE BOOKS!

2 FREE NOVELS
PLUS 2 *FREE GIFTS!*

KIMANI™
ROMANCE

Love's ultimate destination!

Liam Westbrook didn't make his way to the top playing it safe. So when the fast-living British bachelor spies an exotic beauty under a smoldering North Carolina moon, he makes a scandalous proposal. Divorced single mother Maya Alvarez does something totally out of character. She accepts an invitation that leads to a hot summer fling with a seductive stranger. When Maya must return to the real world, will Liam and their pleasure-fueled fantasy end up as only an affair to remember?

Read on for a sneak peek at
PLAYING WITH DESIRE,
the first exciting installment in author Reese Ryan's
PLEASURE COVE series!

"Mr. Westbrook, I'll seat you now." The hostess approached Hot Suit Guy with a menu.

"That's our table, love." The man stood, extending his hand to her.

Her eyes traveled up the sleeve of his expensive suit. *Definitely athletic cut.*

The man was tall, and even more handsome upon closer inspection. *Michael Ealy meets Adam Levine handsome.*

Her heart beat a little faster and a jolt of electricity traveled the length of her spine. She shuddered inwardly. Handsome and charming, and he damn well knew it.

A man like that is bad news.

She had two kids and a divorce decree to prove it. It would be safer to pass on the invitation. And she intended to, because that was just what she did. She made sensible choices. Played it safe. But the man's expectant grin taunted her. Dared her to venture beyond the cozy cocoon of her safe and predictable life.

He's being a gentleman. Why not let him?

Maya placed her hand in his and let him pull her to her feet. Heat radiated up her arm from the warmth of his hand on hers. His clean scent—like freshly scrubbed man, new leather and sin—was captivating.

Maybe sin didn't have a scent, per se. But if it did, it would smell like him, with his mischievous smile and eyes so dark and intense they caused a flutter in her belly whenever she looked into them.

She tucked her hand into the bend of his elbow as he followed the hostess to their table. Maya concentrated on putting one foot in front of the other. The simple feat required all of her concentration.

"Thank you." The words tumbled from her lips the second the hostess left them alone. "It was kind of you to come to my rescue, but I doubt dinner with a random stranger was your plan for tonight. I'll order something to go from the bar and let you get back to your evening." The inflection at the end of the phrase indicated it was a question. She hadn't intended it to be. The thinking part of her brain clearly wasn't the part of her body in control at the moment.

His dark eyes glinted in the candlelight. "My motives aren't as altruistic as you might imagine. The opportunity to dine with a beautiful woman presented itself, so I seized it. I'd much prefer your company to eating alone."

Don't miss PLAYING WITH DESIRE
by Reese Ryan, available March 2017
wherever Harlequin® Kimani Romance™
books and ebooks are sold.